THE REMOTE VIEWER

Fall of the Brotherhood

Book 2

By

Mark A. McCormick

Table of Contents

Dedication

In remembrance of Christian Slade Cunningham.

"The true worth of a man is what he leaves in his wake. It doesn't matter his age, his religion, his background, nor the color of his skin. It's how he spent his time on earth, and how well he was received."

Rest in peace beloved son, brother, and friend.

Preface

Over the course nearly a year, a relative calmness fell across the globe. With the foiled attacks on the United States and the fall of the Brotherhood, terrorism had fallen to an all-time low. However, peace on earth was not to be, at least not in our lifetime.

Terrorism increased to an unprecedented level. Subsequently, beheadings across the globe reached unparalleled proportions.

People from all lifestyles and religions were persecuted and tormented. Not even the terrorists themselves were immune from the threat of beheading if they were unwilling to fight and give their lives. The Brotherhood once again reared its ugly head, and at its helm, a new leader.

He planned to instill fear in all who opposed the Brotherhood and the Muslim ways according to the Koran, or rather, the Koran as he interpreted it. His plan had been very effective at first, but ultimately resulted in a mass exile of people leaving their countries and fleeing for their lives. Many Middle Eastern cities were overrun and fell to the

Brotherhood, resulting in many killed or taken prisoner.

President John Davy's second term ended and with it came the termination of the Stargate project. Stargate, set up on a Presidential finding several years prior, was disbanded.

The Stargate team members reluctantly dispersed and integrated into civilian life. A few remained in the same line of work while others attempted to resume a normal life, and only a small group remained in touch with one another.

Jonas had had enough and longed for the peace-and-quiet lifestyle. Cayce, on the other hand, wanted to get back into her private practice, as well as mend bridges with her relatives, something she had been thinking of doing for a while, but had never quite gotten around to. She remained the only person within the group that knew where Jonas went, and the only one who maintained contact with him.

The investigation into the doomed terrorist attack on the United States by the terrorist group known as the Brotherhood had been ongoing for the past nine months and appeared to be winding to a close.

After several months of being run through the mill by the Senate Oversight Committee, Major Crawford and the newly-former President Davy, as well as several of his former cabinet members, were quite ready for it to end and to put the whole affair behind them.

However, the United Nations and the British Parliament requested Crawford to give a briefing on the event. Allowed to pick the team was to accompany him on the trip, he contacted Cayce, Doc and 5 operatives, the only people of which he knew the whereabouts. As luck would have it, all five agreed to the trip and speaking on behalf of the United States and former President Davy.

With four months to kill before the briefing, Crawford agreed to give everyone a well-deserved vacation for the next three months, at which point they would reconvene to get their presentation together before heading to their first stop: the United Nations in New York.

The time passed quickly, during which the investigation into the incident was completed. The Senate Oversight Committee, after weeks of deliberation, determined that there was no wrongdoing or liability held for the actions taken during the attack.

The eight remaining members reconvened at Crawford's place of residence to sort out the facts and get their presentation ready. The United Nations and Parliament would naturally have several questions to which they would demand answers, and Crawford wanted correct and concise answers to give them.

The remaining four weeks flew by and before they knew it, it was time to leave. After New York, the plan was to fly to Geneva, and then a charter a flight to London.

However, two weeks into their trip the unthinkable happened: after leaving Geneva, the small charter aircraft that was en route to London vanished from radar.

No one has neither seen nor heard from anyone in the group since.

I: Old Wounds

Fog had settled into the cool snow covered Appalachian Mountains. It was early morning; the air was brisk, and you could hear the slightest of sounds for miles as the echoes carried down the hollows and valleys.

In the distance, the sound of an axe head smacking its sharp edge into a waiting piece of wood resonated. *Crack! Crack!* Only the sounds of nature could be heard in between each sound of the wood splitting.

The old rustic cabin was nestled way back off the beaten path. Only a small weather-beaten road lead to the small clearing in which it stood. A man in a drab green parka and a six-month beard stood swinging the axe that had broken the morning silence, occasionally stopping to stack the wood into a pile.

Dressed in full winter camouflage, a figure silently creeped closer and watched as the man continued to chop and stack the wood. The man rested the axe against the wood pile, and began to collect an armload of wood.

With the strange sense that he was being watched, he stopped, turning on the spot to scrutinize the area. The camouflaged figure dropped to the ground for fear of being seen, elevating his head after a few moments to get a quick check the area.

The man had gone. The figure frantically glanced from side to side, and seeing no one, he got up and quickly ran to a better hiding place where he squatted down and waited.

Hours passed and no sound or movement came from inside or around the cabin. Assuming it was safe, the man in the camouflage began to creep up to the side of the cabin. He listened carefully, but heard no sound.

Slowly he crept towards the cabin porch, frequently stopping to glance behind. Once he had circled the building, he stopped. He seemed unsure of what to do next, and decided to move once again.

Suddenly, he felt cold steel on the side of his face and the *click* of the hammer locking back as a voice came from behind him.

"Raise them slowly so I can see them." Slowly and cautiously, he complied as the man searched him for weapons. Upon finding none, he demanded, "Now stand up and turn around. Who are you and what do you want?"

The camouflaged man slowly raised his hands with palms out and removed his hood and ski mask, standing up straight to face a pristine .45 caliber Colt action, 1925 model Smith & Wesson, with hardwood oak handles and etched chrome.

The weapon lowered as the man let out a sigh. "Marrow, you son of a bitch. I could have killed you. What the hell are you doing snooping around up here?" Jonas snapped after a moment.

Jeff Marrow had been his associate at the Stargate Project which disbanded a little over a year prior. Jeff was a close friend and confidant, and a well-rounded psychic in his own right. He was not sure whether to be glad to see him or knock him on his ass for sneaking around.

"Hello Jonas, it's been a while," Jeff replied as he and Jonas shook hands.

"Come on inside so you can tell me why you're up here sneaking around. It's damn cold out here," Jonas stated as he placed the .45 back into its holster and headed for the door. They shed their winter coats inside and Jonas poured two fingers of Gentleman Jack into two hi-ball glasses.

As they sat down Jonas began. "Ok, I'm not going to ask the obvious, such as how you found me. So, I'll jump right to the meat of the question: what the hell you are doing up here?"

Jeff downed a long swig from his glass and gazed at Jonas in thought before responding. "I was sent here to find you and bring you back with me."

This statement took Jonas aback; he sat bemused for a few seconds. "I thought the Stargate Project was finished. Why would I need to go back?"

Jeff rose from his seat and walked to the fireplace. "When was the last time you spoke to Cayce?" he asked.

The mention of Cayce's name quickly got Jonas' attention. He sat up on the edge of his seat. He and Cayce had stayed in touch off and on over the past year. However, the phone calls gradually grew shorter as well as less frequent. "I haven't heard from her in at least a month, maybe two… Why?" Jonas was now getting annoyed with the runaround, as well as alarmed. "Get to the point," he added.

Jeff was now feeling pressured. The corner of his right eye began to twitch as it always did when he got nervous or told a lie. He started to pace. "Two weeks ago, the Major and a group of former Stargate contacts, including Cayce and Doc, traveled to New York and Geneva to deliver a rundown to the United Nations on what took place during the incident last year.

"After Geneva, they were to take a charter flight to London and give the same debrief to the British Parliament. However, about halfway through the flight, the transponder fell off the radar screen." Jeff paused. "No one has seen or heard from anyone in the group since then. A very detailed search was conducted, but albeit with no results, no wreckage, nothing."

He paused once again, swallowing hard. "And then, yesterday a video was posted on the internet." He pulled out a tablet and then sat it in front of Jonas. "I gotta warn you: it's not pretty and very upsetting," he cautioned.

Jonas hesitated to hit the play button, unsure he wanted to see what was going to show up on the little screen. Slowly he reached over and started the video, and the little screen danced to life. Front and center, gagged, tied, and on his knees was Crawford. From the looks of it, he appeared to have been beaten considerably.

Behind him was a man dressed in all black from head to toe holding a long curved knife, the large black flag of the Brotherhood draped on the back wall. Jonas watched in shock; he could not move, nor could he take his eyes away from the little screen.

"I have before me an adversary of the Brotherhood," the man in black declared in near perfect English. "This is what we do to our adversaries." In a swift heart-pounding moment, he reached down and slashed Crawford's throat. His eyes flew open wide; shock and pain rushed out in a voiceless scream as the man in black continued hacking away, until he had severed Crawford's head and his body fell lifeless to the floor.

"My God!" shrieked Jonas as he rose and dashed to the bathroom. He vomited profusely several times. After several minutes, he returned, a look of total disbelief set into his eyes, and face as white as a sheet.

"There's more," Jeff stated. "I'm sorry but you need to watch it."

Jonas glanced at Jeff, took a deep breath, and started the video again. He watched as the man in black held Crawford's head. His gag reflex kicked in again, and he struggled to fight it back.

He watched as the man in black raised the severed head high into the air. "We have more enemies of this faction, and they too will share this fate if our demands are not met." The camera panned left, and on the screen were Cayce and Doc along with several others from the group, each gagged and tied. Trails of tears were streaming down Cayce's face.

"I give you ten days to free four of which you hold prisoner in Guantanamo; you know their names. I also want the man they call 'the viewer,' the man who helped to take the lives of Oman and his men, as well as the lives of many other innocent men, women and children. Ten days to send me the prisoners and this viewer, or in the name of Allah and Oman the martyr, they too will suffer the same fate as your Major, one for each day over ten you make me wait."

The screen faded out to black, and Jeff reached over and shut off the tablet. Jonas sat reeling in total disbelief. His hands were shaking and his mind was sprinting out of control. *"My God...the look in his eyes..."* he thought out loud. "Those fucking animals."

Jonas knew that Cayce, Doc, and the others would be next if the demands were not met. However, he also knew the President would never give into these demands.

"This is why you have got to come back with me Jonas. We have to do something to save them," Jeff stated as he paced between Jonas and the fireplace.

Jonas snapped out of his thoughts and peeked up at Jeff, *"'Oman the martyr?' We made him a fucking martyr?!* What in the hell is wrong with those people over there? And where is Mahoney? Does he know?"

Jeff nodded. "Yes. He's the one that sent me here, and he's waiting for word from me. We needed to get you onboard before figuring out what to do next. So are you onboard? Should I call him so we can get going?"

Jonas leapt to his feet as that proverbial taste for revenge once again surged through his veins, saturating his mouth, mind, and body with the taste for blood. He gave Jeff a sideways look. "You know I am. Crawford, Cayce, and the whole team from Stargate saved my ass, and I owe every single member my life."

He grabbed a suitcase and rapidly packed it, tossing in only the necessities and clothes for a week. Before he closed the lid, he chucked in his .45 caliber and a box of shells, and then grabbed his coat. With nothing else being said he headed for the door.

Kyle Mahoney was a tall muscularly built man in his late fifties, and he had been Crawford's right-hand man and confidante during the Stargate Project years. When he first came on board, he had no experience in the ESP or psychic field. He was a former Light Bird Colonel and Special Ops leader, and that was his forte. Crawford had brought him into Stargate for his leadership abilities and training in tactics. However, over the years, he had learned a vast amount of information from the Major and its team members.

Now with the Major gone, Mahoney was the head of the team, so to speak. Government sanctioned or not they were still a team, and everyone involved had accepted that fact.

Mahoney had devoted the morning to contacting what remained of the group that he trusted, arranging travel plans, and trying to get everyone back to the old Stargate facility where he needed them to be.

Thus far, he had been able to contact a total of nine from the group, everyone except for Jonas. He had made it hard for anyone to contact him, mostly because he wanted it that way.

"I am headed for the great unknown; never to be harassed again, so don't bother looking for me." These were the last dramatic words he spoke as he left the group and Stargate. No one had heard from or seen him since, except for Cayce.

Mahoney had sent out Jeff Marrow to locate and bring him back, knowing that if anyone could locate him, it was Jeff. He hoped that word would come soon, sure that there would be no question of him coming back once he found out Cayce was involved. And of course, he was right.

After the hour-long trek out of the forest, and another two-hour's drive through the snow-covered mountains, Jonas and Jeff had finally reached the airport. It was a small commuter airport with a short runway. When Jeff had landed, he requested that the aircraft be refueled and ready for him when he returned, and it was.

They climbed into the Cessna 182. Jeff fired it up and they taxied out to the runway, shortly taking off and on their way. Jeff happened to glance over at Jonas and noticed the white knuckles clutching the Jesus handle.

"Have you ever flown in one of these?" he asked.

Jonas kept nervously staring straight ahead. "No! These little Buddy Holly aircraft scare the hell out of me."

Jeff smiled, fighting the urge to laugh. "We'll only be flying for a couple of hours, and besides, the worst is over. I absolutely despise taking off in snow. In the meantime, I'll fill you in on the details that I'm aware of, and a few I'm guessing. Maybe that will help pass the time."

Jonas nodded. "Good idea."

During the flight, he told Jonas everything he knew, and Jonas countered him with a barrage of questions. Most he could answer, but some he could not. Jonas wanted nothing more than to trip into Cayce to check on her, most of all to try to find out where she and the others were taken, but he needed more information.

"They know about you Jonas," Jeff stated as if reading his mind. "If they were somehow able to lock onto your thoughts or Cayce's or any other member's in the group, they would know the instant you tried to trip into her or any of the others. These men don't seem like the run of the mill terrorist, and it wouldn't surprise me if they have set a trap with what they know about you."

Jonas recalled China: how she was able to invade his mind, inflicting so much pain. Putting the lives of any of the others else in danger was not worth the risk. He had no choice but to wait until they got back to the old Stargate facility. Once there, he hoped he could get more information before risking a trip. The thought of losing another loved one to these terrorists was killing him. It would not happen, not as long as he had a say.

In the small township of Al-Salman in southern Iraq, two armed men stood guard outside the front and back entries to an old rundown warehouse. Several others guarded the roof and grounds surrounding the warehouse within the fenced in compound, securing the missing Stargate team members, who were being held captive in separate rooms from each other.

Voices echoed through the hallways and off the walls of the warehouse. A faint yet noticeable whimper was barely audible beneath it all. Cayce, gagged and bound, sat on the floor in a corner of a vacant room, sobbing quietly

II. The Black Sheik

Six hours before the video posted on the internet, and only moments after the event with Crawford had taken place, a mass of three hundred armed men, most with automatic weapons, gathered around a small platform just outside the old warehouse in Al-Salman.

Without warning, the roll-up door opened on the side of the building. The crowd moved silently as a man dressed fully in black walked out to the platform. He paused as he looked down at the ground with his hands behind his back.

From the top of the platform, he slowly raised his head and gazed out over the crowd. A silent tension filled the air, before the black sheik yelled out in Arabic, *"Death to the infidels and praise be to Allah!"* He thrust his hands high into the air, holding Crawford's head in one hand and the Koran in the other.

Immediately, the mob went wild, hooting and yelling, raising their weapons into the air and firing shots. The black sheik stood there for a full minute, then flung Crawford's head to the ground in front of the platform.

He proceeded to join in the celebration for several minutes before turning to re-enter the warehouse. The door rolled closed while the crowd continued to celebrate. Inside, the black sheik began to disrobe while giving orders to several men around him.

"We must keep the morale up. The United States will not take what we have done lying down, and we must be ready," he stated as he removed his turban and threw it on a desk. "However, this time we will be ready for them. Tell my gifted ones I wish to meet with them. We must begin our plan to counter these psychics the United States uses, in order to turn the tables in our favor." One of the men standing next to the sheik nodded, bowing his head as he exited the room.

Jonas and Jeff arrived at the former headquarters of Stargate. The gate was unlocked, and the place look even more run down than Jonas previously remembered. Jeff drove to the back of the building, and right up to the old roll-up door. He shut off the ignition and proceeded to get out.

"What? No elevator ride?" Jonas queried, referring to the car elevator inside that scared the hell out of him on his first visit to Stargate.

Jeff turned, hi face void of all expression. "No power. Once we left the building, it was completely shut down."

A small side door opened, and out walked Kyle Mahoney. "Come on in guys we have a lot to cover," he shouted as he motioned for them, "And time is getting shorter by the minute." He turned back through the doorway as Jonas and Jeff followed.

The three of them went down three flights of stairs to the level where the lab had once been. Mahoney had rigged up a portable generator to supply power to most of the sublevel floor. "Watch your step. When they cleaned this place out they made a real mess of things," Mahoney announced.

They reached the old cafeteria. Except for a display Mahoney had set up to put information and a few chairs, the room was completely empty.

"Is this it?" questioned Jonas. "I mean no one else is coming?"

Mahoney turned to him. "Yes, we have more coming. Albeit not as many as I had hoped. It seems a few have disappeared from the map, a few have married and have families, and unfortunately, some are no longer with the living. But, counting you we have ten, and by day's end everyone should be here."

Jonas walked to the board and viewed the pictures and notes hanging from it. "Any idea where they're keeping them?" he asked.

"Not yet, but I'm expecting a phone call soon and hopefully a little help will come with it," responded Mahoney.

Jonas began to pace around the room deep in thought. "So they know about me; that much is fact. But how *much* do they know? How long can Doc, Cayce, and the rest of them hold out from telling them more?"

He stopped and turned to Kyle and Jeff. "You do know they will torture them for information, don't you?" He noticeably began getting more agitated during this process. "I swear to God if one of them touches a single hair on her head, I'll put five in the ground."

"OK...OK... Calm down; we all feel the same way." Mahoney asserted. "We have the best psychics in the business, and I'm more than confident we'll get to them."

Jonas shot him a look. "You had better be right! Time is not our friend right now. They're a long ways away, and we need to get there now!"

Jonas was known for having a short fuse, and the team members always gave him a wide birth when he got mad or frustrated about something.

"Do you think it's feasible to allow Jonas try to trip into one of them?" Jeff interjected.

Mahoney gave this additional thought before responding. "I'm not sure we should risk it as of now. Jumping the gun and allowing any psychic contact at this point could cost someone their life, especially when we don't know if they have found a way to monitor or block the process. I think it's best to wait."

Jonas chimed in. "How soon before we can get over there?"

Mahoney threw a serious, but quizzical glance at Jonas. "First, we need to find out where *there* is, but as soon as the rest of us get here, we leave."

Jonas walked towards Mahoney and Jeff. "I've been attempting to perfect an alternate way of viewing, or – well – an alternate way for *me* that is. I've tried it out on short distances, and it works fine. However, my attempts over a long range have been shaky at best, and I'm not sure I can do it. It depends on how far away they are."

He paused for effect and then resumed. "What I've been attempting to do is view outside the person's body, to get an overhead view, looking down and around the person in question. I do this by tripping into the person only for a second or two and then making the jump out."

Mahoney, now intrigued, piped up in response. "So what you're saying is you're trying to view like a normal remote viewer would, correct?" Jonas nodded in agreement.

Mahoney stood in deep thought and slightly nodding his head. "This could be our ace in the hole," he muttered, seemingly not noticing he was speaking aloud. "Wait here I'll be right back." He turned with his cell phone in hand as he left the room, leaving Jonas and Jeff standing there with confused looks on their faces as they watched him leave.

Cayce sat tied and gagged in her small cell. Her hands were numb from the tight bindings, and she was parched from lack of water. It had been four days since she and the rest of the group were taken prisoner, and small scraps of food along with a half cup of water twice a day were all they had given her each day.

She struggled with her bindings, attempting to free herself to no avail. The room was cold, and the air was stagnant with the smell of animal musk and unwashed bodies. In the distance she could hear footsteps and voices. Frozen in fear, she listened as the sound of footsteps ceased and the talking continued.

After a minute or two, the talking ceased, and the footsteps began again. They got louder as they drew closer, and she began to panic, trying to scoot further away from the direction of the sound.

Without warning, the door flung open and someone entered. Cayce could not tell who or how many, but she could tell it was more than one. Someone grabbed her from behind and lifted her by her arms, which were still tied behind her back.

She squealed from both fright and pain as she was yanked up and roughly pushed down into a chair. One of the men stood behind her with his hands on her shoulders as a second began to question her.

"Who you work for?" the second man asked in broken English. Though she still was still blindfolded, she could tell that the man was at her eye level; she could feel his breath on her face, and the stench was revolting. "Tell me about this viewer person."

She remained silent. *"Answer me bitch!"* A resounding slap echoed within the room as the man's open hand connected with the side of her head.

The man resumed, once again getting down into her face. "You are not in United States anymore. You are bound by our laws, our ways. Here you are nothing. Foolish American. You understand me?" Another resounding slap connected against the side of her head, this time harder. She let out a whimper as the pain magnified.

"You will be treated as far less than one of our own women," the man continued. "You are an infidel and are lower as such. We will shave that nice yellow hair from your head, and you will wear the rags of a peasant female. You will be our servant to do with as we desire."

She shook her head and squirmed in the chair. Muffled wailing came from behind the gag in her mouth.

The stench of the man's breath was once again in her face. "You will regret the day you ever crossed the Brotherhood. Your life will be hell until we decide to end it for you." He let out a petrifying laugh that sent a chill down her spine as the hands that restrained her were removed.

She was snatched up by her hair and lifted up out of the chair like a bag of feed. The rough hands flung her onto the floor and into the corner. She lay there motionless for several moments while she listened to the men leave the room and close the door. All at once, the gravity of her situation hit her, and she bellowed out an uncontrollable wail.

At the other end of the warehouse, the black sheik concluded a meeting with the people he considered his gifted ones. "I will distribute a prisoner to each of you. You will watch them in pairs and will change out every twelve hours. Your job is to prevent anyone outside from making contact with our guests. If an attempt does happen to be made, I want to know immediately. Do you understand?" Everyone within the group quickly stood, voicing their support in Arabic. He motioned for them to sit. "The list will be up within the hour. I know you will not let me down," he concluded.

He left the room and returned to his small office inside the warehouse, where he met with the three men who had paid a visit to Cayce.

"She didn't say a word. Only a few whimpers," explained the third man, who had merely observed the interrogation from the corner of the room.

The black sheik nodded. "As I expected. Did you tell her of our plans?"

A shorter man with the blue eyes, the one who happened to have done the interrogation, replied, "Yes, and from her response, I don't think she liked what we had to say." He smirked.

"Good...good. We will now wait until morning, and then we will do as we have told her: shave her head and add a few more bruises to her pretty little face. After that, we make another video. This will assure the United States that we are not to be taken lightly. We will act if they do not comply."

"What of the others?" the first man asked.

"Make them regret. Do with them as you will, just keep them alive… for now," the black sheik responded enigmatically.

After lifting off from Jacksonville International Airport, Jonas and the remaining nine members of the Stargate Project reviewed what was known of the terrorist.

Mahoney started the meeting. "From what my sources tell me, the Brotherhood has split into several factions, and due to that, they do not have the number or strength they once had. My source believes the new leader's ideals have caused many within the group to doubt his leadership."

"What do we know of this new leader?" Jonas inquired.

"Not much," Mahoney explained. "He appears to have come out of nowhere. However, my source says that chances are high he has always been involved in the Brotherhood, and that he somehow has worked his way into the head position."

Mahoney continued, as Jeff pulled out a laptop. "We do have a bit of support, though I can't say who or where. They are going to try to help us by running Intel from the States. They are, at this time, running a facial scan of the man in black from the video. With any luck we can nail down who he is, but until then we need to locate where they are concealing our friends."

Jonas piped up once again. "I'll know when we are getting close." He paused glancing around at everyone. "I know I can't constantly view though their eyes for fear of getting caught, but if I'm close enough and able to trip into them for just a couple of seconds, I may be able to see around them."

"That's what I'm banking on, Jonas," Mahoney countered.

"So where do we start looking?" Jeff queried as he pulled up Google Maps.

"Well," Mahoney started, "the main Islamic states that the Brotherhood operate out of – the ones that we know to have training camps, as well as troop buildups – are Afghanistan, Iraq, and Pakistan. My plan is this:

we split into groups and each take a state. Any leads as to where they might be will be reported back to me."

Mahoney paused in thought. "I will stay in Dubai and coordinate operations from there. My sources will try to manipulate the satellites and drones to view the area and confirm activity. Once we have a solid lead with photos backing it, we will converge on that area. Any questions so far?"

Jeff raised his hand. Mahoney smiled and shook his head. "Just speak up. You don't need to raise your hand." Jeff's face turned red as he shyly lowered his hand.

"Sorry, habit," he replied, embarrassed. "You said that you will coordinate out of Dubai. How do we contact you, and how will we get to our respective states and complete the investigation without being caught? "

Mahoney reached around to the seat behind him and pulled out a large black case, opening and turning it around so everyone could see the contents. Inside was an assortment of electronic gadgets, including a DVD recording camera, a laptop, and a microphone.

Everyone glanced at each other confused. "You're going as television journalist," Mahoney clarified, "and you're there to report on the effects of the Brotherhood since their reign began." Flickers of enlightenment filled everyone's eyes as they nodded.

Smiling he continued. "I have also set up a contact in each state to help you get around, acting as your interpreter." He handed out folders to each member. "I want you to study these and memorize the information in them. I expect you to know it by heart by the time we land in London for refueling, because at that point we dump everything that says anything but a television journalist.

"As to how you will contact me, I will have a telepath with me at all times, so just send your thoughts. In an emergency, such as, God forbid, you lose your telepath, send me an e-mail or text, but *only* if it's an emergency." He paused, his face serious to ensure the group understood the gravity of his words. "Let's get to it. We have five hours before we land in London and seven until we get to Dubai."

Jonas returned to his seat and opened the folder. Inside was a picture of a young man, maybe in his early twenties. The first typed out page described who the man was. Aljeb Aljagin was Iraqi-born and American-educated. He would be the point of contact and interpreter that Mahoney had mentioned.

He continued reading through the contents of the folder. It outlined several points as to where there may be activity and conceivable locations where they could be hiding the former members of Stargate. It also gave a rendezvous place and time to meet. It appeared he was getting Iraq, and the rendezvous point was a small town by the name of Rafha, just inside the northern border to Saudi Arabia

The government of the United Arab Emirates had reluctantly agreed to fly each of the groups from Dubai via commuter aircraft, getting them as close as possible to the rendezvous points. This had taken Mahoney and his contact a considerable amount of time and persuasion to accomplish. In Jonas' case, it would be Kuwait. From there, he and whoever his partner was would catch a ride to the rendezvous point.

Jonas studied the contents of the folder for several hours and committed them to memory. It had encompassed about every scenario that they could run into, including capture, which he was determined to avoid, no matter what.

After a while, he decided to stop and give his mind a rest. It had already been a long day, and that, coupled with the fact that he was going to lose eight hours thanks to jetlag, made it seem even longer. He decided it was best to squeeze in a snooze while he could.

III: Silent Partners

Jonas was jolted awake as the aircraft touched down at London's Heathrow Airport. He glanced at his watch; it was midnight, or rather 0500 hours London time, and the morning of the third day since the video arrived. The aircraft taxied to the terminal where it parked for refueling.

"Okay everyone, get out and stretch your legs, and meet back here in thirty. Don't be late," Mahoney announced. Everyone slowly got out of their seats and made for the exit.

Jonas made his way inside the airport terminal and found a newsstand. He wanted to see if any information had been picked up by the news and if so, what it said. Skimming several of the papers, he found not one word about the abduction or the beheading, which he found to be very odd considering it happened right after a United Nations meeting.

On the aircraft, Mahoney made a sweep through the aircraft, and supervised the refueling. Soon they would be ready to leave once again.

Eventually, everyone returned and boarded. The aircraft started up and taxied out to the runway, and within minutes, they were airborne. Jonas noticed that several items had been removed from the aircraft during the stop, including the luggage, all the folders, as well as the personal laptop computers. Each team member had only one suitcase left onboard, which appeared to each have been gone through as well. He made his way to the back of the aircraft where Mahoney was sitting and sat in the chair beside him.

Mahoney turned in his seat to face Jonas. "Question?" he asked.

Jonas sat looking straight ahead in thought. "I checked the newspapers while we were refueling, and something is puzzling me." Mahoney sat listening expressionless as Jonas continued. "There was no mention in any of the papers about any of this. Why?"

Mahoney nodded his head. "Parliament and the United Kingdom squelched the story before it could be announced or printed. It was done per request of the United States, or well… someone of importance within the United States," he added.

Jonas thought for a moment and already knowing the answer asked, "Am I allowed to know who this someone is? Is it your source?"

Mahoney shook his head. "It's best if this someone stays anonymous at this juncture. If we are successful, he or she may decide to reveal themselves, but that's their call."

Jonas nodded his acceptance. "Well, whoever they are, they must really have clout."

"That they do," Mahoney replied, "that they do." After a brief moment of silence he asked, "Anything else I can do for you?"

Jonas thought for a second. "I take it you haven't decided who's getting paired with who yet? Do we get a choice of partners?"

Mahoney grinned and chuckled. "I'm still kicking it around because a few of the people we have are not very experienced in the field. With that being said, I need to make sure I pair them up with someone that can support them if needed. I'll have it figured out by the time we land."

Jonas again nodded. "Ok, I have just one more thing: my .45? Where is it?"

A large smile came across Mahoney's face as he replied, "It's in a safe place."

Jonas slightly titled his head quizzically to the right. "Just make sure that it is. You know that weapon means a lot to me." He got up, headed back to his seat, sat down, and began thinking about Cayce.

What she must be going through, he thought to himself. "Don't worry baby, I coming," he stated softly under his breath, and turning to the window, he sighed as he watched dawn break outside.

The aircraft finally touched down in Dubai at 0936 hours, Dubai time. By the time the team cleared customs and found three cabs, it was 1005 Dubai time. The skies were clear with a temperature of 47 degrees. Subsequently, no one on the team except for Mahoney expected it to be as cold as it was.

Twenty minutes later, they reached the U.S. embassy. They approached the marine guard at the gate, and Mahoney requested to meet with the ambassador.

"Do you have an appointment?" the guard asked.

"No," Mahoney replied. "Nevertheless, it's of the utmost importance that I get in to speak to him."

The guard looked over Mahoney's paperwork and military identification. "One moment please," he replied as he turned and went into the booth and picked up the phone. After a few minutes, he returned. "If you will please follow the walkway to the doors, someone will be waiting."

Mahoney thanked the guard, and they headed off down the sidewalk. Eventually they came to a door where another marine guard stood waiting. "Welcome the U.S. embassy sir," the staff Sargent said while holding open the door. "If you and your team will please go to the counter, we will get you logged in and on to see the ambassador."

After signing in and handing over their passports, as well as answering a barrage of questions regarding firearms and passport history, they were passed through to the next room. There, another young marine corporal stood waiting, and took them to a small conservatory outside the ambassador's office.

Other than the door they entered by, there was only one other door on the far side of the room. As they sat on the plush leather sofa waiting, Mahoney stood up. "I want you all to stay here while I speak to the ambassador." Pointing to Jonas he added, "Except for you."

Jonas taken aback by this could only manage to nod his head and ask, "Me sir? Why me?"

Mahoney smiled. "Personally, I feel for your own wellbeing and interest, you need to be there. Besides, you may have something to add into this meeting."

Jonas, now even more confused raised his eyebrows. "Ok sir, if you say so."

Mahoney nodded. "I do."

After fifteen minutes, the door on the far side opened, and out walked an attractive auburn-haired woman who appeared to be in her forties, though Jonas felt she was much older than she appeared.

"Colonel Mahoney?" She asked as she approached. Mahoney and Jonas rose from their seats. "If you will follow me, the ambassador will see you now." She turned and walked back to the doorway.

Mahoney and Jonas followed her into a small office with a desk, computer, and several filing cabinets. She continued to the door on the opposite side of the room and walked in, holding the door as Mahoney and Jonas entered.

"Colonel Mahoney. Welcome, please come in and have a seat." The ambassador uttered as they entered. "I must say this is a surprise; I rarely get unannounced visitors." Reaching out his hand, he added, "I am Ambassador Joel Izsak. Can I get you anything to drink?"

Mahoney reached out, grasped the ambassador's hand, and shook it while replying, "I'm Colonel Kyle Mahoney and this is Jonas Lux and not for me thanks." He motioned towards Jonas, who reiterated the same.

"Please, sit and tell me what I can do for you." Ambassador Izsak smiled. Mahoney and Jonas took seats across the desk from the ambassador, who sat back into his seat and waited.

"Ambassador, we… or *I* need your help," Mahoney began. "I know you're aware of the kidnapping of our U.S. members, and the beheading of at least one that we know of at this point."

The ambassador nodded showing no emotion and sat forward in his chair, placing his elbows on the desk while tapping his fingertips together. Taking a deep breath, he began. "Yes colonel, I am very aware of what has taken place over the past week, and I am also aware that you have come here looking for help."

Mahoney looked at him quizzically. "Pardon me for asking sir, but who have you spoken to about our mission?"

The ambassador sat back into his chair once again and drew a deep breath, then exhaled. "I think you know," he replied as he opened the drawer to his lower right. "It's not every day I get a phone call from a former president asking a favor."

Mahoney slid back into his seat a little confused, but not surprised. "So former president Davy called you? What did he ask? That is, if you don't mind me asking."

"Me? Mind? Why should I mind? The call was about you and your mission. Why would I mind you asking about something you already know?" From the drawer, he pulled a large manila folder, which he laid on his desk.

Jonas, following the conversation, finally realized who Mahoney's contact was. He pondered the former president's reason for helping as he continued to listen.

"I have known John Davy for a long time; he appointed me to my first embassy job in Sudan years ago. When he asked me for my help, I figured I owed him that much. Besides, I knew Major Crawford; he was a good man. Nonetheless, I advised John that I am no longer beholding to him, as he is no longer the sitting president. In spite of this, I told him I would help, but I will not jeopardize my position or the interest of the United States to do so."

Ambassador Izsak slid the envelope across the desk to Mahoney. "This much I have done, and as for any other help you may need, let's just take it one step at a time shall we?"

Mahoney took the envelope and opened it. Inside were several media passes and ID's as well as documentation to support them. "Take them to the third floor with your team. They will take pictures and add them to the ID badges for you."

The ambassador stood up. "I also have you a place here in Dubai that you can work out of during your stay. Here is the address and keys. It's my safe house, and it's yours for as long as you need it."

Mahoney reached over and took the keys along with the slip of paper with the address, offering a hand to the ambassador, thanking him as he shook his hand.

"Just keep me informed of what's happening so I don't get blindsided. Call me at this number anytime, and good luck to you," the ambassador stated, verifying his commitment to help.

"I will, and thank you again," Mahoney replied, as he and Jonas turned to find the attractive auburn-haired woman standing by the door waiting. She directed them to the elevator where they got on and went to get their pictures taken.

An hour and a half later, they arrived at the safe house and unloaded the equipment. Mahoney was just about to go outside to call Davy when Jonas caught him. "So, it's Davy?" Jonas remarked. "Why, may I ask, is he willing to go out on a limb to help us?"

Mahoney stopped dead in his tracks and turned. "How well did you get to know Cayce?" he questioned.

This question completely caught Jonas off guard. "Cayce? What's Cayce got to do with the former President?"

"What I'm asking is… How much do you know of her family?"

Still confused and wondering where this line of questioning was leading. He thought for a second and replied. "Not much we never really talked about them. Why are you asking me this?"

"Well, Cayce is his niece; his sister is her mother. That's why he's helping. It's personal to him. He would do anything to try to save her and the rest of the group's lives. That's also why I wanted you in on the meeting with the Ambassador." Mahoney stated with frustration note in his tone.

Jonas was dumbfounded. He never put it together: why she never talked about her family and why she deflected any questions about them. "Son of a bitch."

"Now if you will excuse me, I need to go and call him to let him know we are here and see if he has anything for us." Mahoney turned and walked outside with phone in hand.

Jonas was stunned for several seconds before he walked back into the living area. He could not find words to speak and could not believe what he had just heard. However, he could definitely understand why the former president was involved.

IV: New Message

Al-Salman warehouse, 0600 hours. Cayce was startled awake by screams of agony echoing off the walls outside her door. They made her put in earbuds to cut her off from another psychic reading her mind, and she could barely hear it through the music.

The shrieks were almost indistinguishable, but she was sure she recognized Doc's voice. *What are they doing to him? Oh God, please; I can't take this!* she thought to herself, as she tried to slide further away from the door.

Cowering in the corner, she wondered if she was next. An eternity passed before the whaling stopped and all was quiet. Suddenly, she thought she heard footsteps. "Please pass me by…Please, please, please…" Cayce whispered to herself under her breath.

The door crashed open as it hit the wall behind it. She screamed from fright, still bound, gagged, and blindfolded. She tried once more to slide further from the doorway.

Just as before, she was lifted from behind by her arms and sat into a chair. She sat whimpering beneath the gag, repeating, *"Please don't hurt me! Please don't! Please!"* The blindfold was ripped from her head and the early morning sun streaming through the one and only small window was blinding. It was the first time in days she had seen daylight.

There were four men: three in front of her, one behind. One of the three in the front was stepping back out the doorway. Of the two in front of her, one was shorter with a black beard and piercing blue eyes. The other stood by the door and was much taller. He also had a beard, but it was reddish in color.

She could not see the man behind her, nor did she ever hear him say anything. She glanced around the room; it was small, and she figured it to be approximately twelve by twelve. The taller man said something in Arabic she did not understand, and the shorter man walked up to her and slapped her hard on the cheek.

The force of the slap caused her head to reel to one side, causing the earplugs to fall from her ears. As he had done before, the shorter man got close to Cayce's face.

She could smell the stench of his breath and fought off the urge to gag. "Are you not glad to see us again?" he asked as he continued to breathe into her face. "We have come to fulfill what we said we would do, and you will now be ours. You will shed your clothes and we will shave your pretty yellow hair from your head as we said we would."

Cayce glared at the shorter man with hatred in her eyes. The man noticed and smacked her once again, and once more, her head snapped to the side. Cayce was overcoming her fear and was getting pissed.

She was not going to let these bastards treat her like a slave. She would not bow down to their wishes; she would rather die first. She straightened up and faced the shorter man, and in her anger she yelled out through the gag. *"Eat shit, you asshole!"*

Shock replaced the smug look on the man's face, and before she could say anything else, he hit her closed fist in the mouth. She was knocked over in the chair onto her back. Her head smacked the dirt floor and she went unconscious.

Jeff Marrow, along with three other psychics from the group, were having breakfast when a vision hit all four of them simultaneously. Jeff began twitching from left to right, his eyes moved around with a dead gaze as if following something.

After, a minute or two, they each came out of their trancelike states. Instantly, Jeff rose from his seat and dashed out of the room in search of Mahoney.

Mahoney was outside walking the grounds and was on the phone with the Davy. He noticed Jeff yelling his head off as he came streaking out of the house. Growing concerned, he spoke into the phone, "Hold on a minute sir, something's going on here. I'll get right back to you."

After finishing the sprint, Jeff was so out of breath he could not speak. *"V - Vis - Vision!"* he finally got out, as he stood there with his hands on his knees trying to catch his breath.

"A vision. You had a vision?" Mahoney echoed, as Jeff nodded his head. "Come on. Back inside." He grabbed Jeff's arm and led him back into the house. Inside, the other three Stargate members were discussing what had happened when Mahoney and Jeff entered the room.

They all began talking at once and making no sense to Mahoney. "Ok! Ok! Calm down!" Mahoney demanded. "Did you all have the same vision?"

Jeff, who had finally caught his breath, replied, "We haven't discussed it between each other yet. As soon as I came out of it, I ran to find you."

"Ok, I see. Let's go in here and then I want each one of you, one at a time, to tell me about your visions." He turned and entered a room to the left. Everyone followed and he closed the door after everyone had entered. "Now, one at a time, starting with you Jeff, tell me what happened."

Jeff began. "We were all sitting at the table eating and going over a few things, and the next thing I knew I was feeling a great amount of pain on the side of my face, not just once, but twice. There was something else too… but I couldn't quite get what it was before I lost the signal. It was gone."

The other three gave their accounts of what they had experienced, and their accounts were all almost exact with one exception. Jeff was the only one that sensed there was something else, something he couldn't grasp, and it was nagging at him.

He vowed to work on the vision and attempt to figure out whatever it was. He would stay at it until he was either sure he could get it or not.

"Alright, please let me know as soon as you figure it out. I need to get everyone together and put this out along with other information." Jeff and the other three headed out to round up the rest of the members.

"We have new developments that will affect how we go about our mission." Mahoney stated as they all met in the dining area. "My source is about 75 percent sure that our people are being held somewhere in Iraq. However, we will need to confirm this information on our own."

Jeff rose from his seat and spread a map of Iraq onto the dining table. Mahoney drew a circle around two areas and continued. "These are the two places my source says have the most recent activity to date." Everyone leaned over to get a good look at the map.

"The first is the town of Al-Kasrah." he pointed to the first circle on the map he had drawn. "The second is here: the town of Al Salmon." Everyone gazed again at the map.

After a few seconds, he continued. "Al-Kasrah is a known training site for the Brotherhood. The United

States has been watching it for years now. Unfortunately, they are unable to do anything about it because the Iraqi officials refuse to admit that the Brotherhood is training people there. I personally believe we should go in and clean house. Fuck 'em all!

"At any rate, anywhere from three to five hundred armed men, woman, and children are training there at any given time. It would be an ideal place to hold hostages. My sources are, at this time, trying to reposition the satellites and get high-altitude drones in the air on the areas in question. Hopefully, this will confirm whether or not they're being held there."

Jonas sat listening for the most part, but finally chimed in after a while. "What makes them 75 percent sure that this could be the place? Being that we are going to concentrate on only Iraq, does this mean that we will be in larger groups?"

"Good questions and I have an answer for each," Mahoney responded. "On the day of the beheading, large groups of personnel were witnessed in both areas. At each area, they were firing their weapons into the air like they were celebrating. This was confirmed by satellite imaging using infrared and drone photos. Oddly enough the weapons being fired at both locations were simultaneous and shortly after the beheading."

"I see; that is odd." he noted and sat back listening.

"As for your second question, Mahoney resumed, "yes, we will be in slightly larger groups, but only by one person. There will be three groups of four, not counting the interpreter. I think more than that will raise too many questions."

"Have you decided who will be with whom yet?" Jeff questioned.

"Yes I have, and as soon as this briefing is finished I will assign each of you to a group. Now, let me finish, and I will answer more questions at that time."

The group fell silent and Mahoney continued. "As for the town of Al Salmon, it's fairly insignificant in terms of a threat, but as I noted before, there was a vast increase of personnel in the area on the day of the beheading, as well as the weapon firing along the same time as the firing in Al-Kasrah. In light of this, it's considered a possible place of interest."

Mahoney glanced over the silent group. "Now, are there any questions about what I have just covered?" The group remained silent. *"Good!* Now, I want to talk specifics, and I will start with Al-Kasrah first."

He then opened up his laptop and brought up Google maps, locating Al-Kasrah on it and zoomed in to ground level. "The Brotherhood training camp is located here on the north side of the town." He pointed to a small group of buildings on a large piece of land with a barricade built around them.

"As you can see they have watchtowers all along the perimeter of the camp. My guess is that the line of sight would be around fifteen to twenty miles from each point. As you can also see, they have several armored vehicles within the compound along with several armed guards as to how many were not sure."

"Good God!" Robert Preston declared in total shock. "Are we to assume that we're going to go through all of that to rescue our other team members?" Jonas first laid eyes on Robert during his first tour through the Stargate facility. Robert had been with Crawford and Stargate for almost as long as Mahoney had been.

"No," Mahoney replied. "As I said before our mission has changed. An hour ago, I spoke to my source, and what he told me leads me to believe that the United States is in the process of prepping a plan to extract the hostages. Our part is to locate and direct them, so that if and when that plan is put into effect, they can be extracted."

"So we just sit on our haunches until then?" Jonas responded with disbelief in his tone.

Mahoney shook his head. "You know better than that. No; we will do as planned to try to locate them and that alone will take time to do." Everyone once again fell silent as Mahoney continued. "Now, let's move on to the other target Al Salmon."

Again, he went to Google maps and brought up the ground view of the town of Al Salmon, and he resumed. "Here we have a warehouse at the edge of town. As you can see, it's much smaller and with less fortification than Al-Kasrah.

"That being said, it doesn't mean it will be an easier target. We don't know for sure what's in that warehouse. It could be weapons of mass destruction or nothing at all. Our people could be in there… or not, but we need to find out."

Inside the warehouse, Cayce was once again being manhandled by the three men that had already visited her twice. She was badly bruised and battered. They had cut off all her hair, made her strip in front of them, and put on the tattered rags as clothing.

Although they had removed the gag, blindfold, and earplugs, her hands were rebound behind her back. She was taken to another room where the Brotherhood flag was hanging from the back wall and made her kneel down in front of the flag with her back to it.

She saw the camera and four men behind it. Tears began to stream down her face as she thought, *This is it. I'm going to die, right here, and right now... Oh God, help me.*

V: The Chameleon

Mahoney had just broken off the briefing when Jeff and the other psychics came rushing back into the dinner area. "Sir, we've had another episode and someone's in trouble." Jeff burst out. "All of us got the exact same words at the same time."

"What words? And from whom?" Mahoney asked.

"I think it was Cayce. She sounded desperate and panicked, and she sounded pretty sure her time is running out. I'm positive it was her," Jeff stated breathlessly.

Mahoney sat quietly for a minute considering what he had been told. "We can't tell Jonas about this. I can't have him running off like he did the last time he got bad news, so keep this between us, understand?"

"Sir," Jeff continued, "the more this happens, the more I'm convinced that they have found a way to block not only us getting to our people, but also vice versa. It just seems odd that we only get impressions when they're under extreme duress."

"Agreed, but let's keep the channels open, it's the only leads we've got right now." Mahoney countered as concern swept over his face.

The men returned Cayce to her tiny room after 20 minutes. They replaced the earbuds and music, and locked her back in with her psychic guard. She did not understand why they did not kill her, but she was grateful.

The best she could figure is that they were using her to get the United States to comply. She did not know how right she was, for thirty minutes later the video was posted on the internet.

It was 1130 hours on the morning of the fourth day. Back in the safe house, Mahoney had divided everyone into groups and they were getting ready to go. They needed to catch their flight and meet the interpreter at the rendezvous point.

Jonas was paired up with a psychic and a telepath, and with their interpreter, there would be four of them. They had three hours to reach the rendezvous point, which for everyone involved, was the small town of Rafha.

It would take two hours just to get to Rafha from Kuwait City by automobile. They only had an hour and a half to spare between getting to Kuwait City and then finding transportation once there. Mahoney had spent most of the morning on the phone with his source trying to finalize the plans, and called a meeting in the lounge room once he was finished.

Jonas was in his room packing up the things he knew he would need, and was the only person not notified of the meeting. Mahoney needed to talk to the rest of the group before Jonas joined them.

Everyone sat waiting in the lounge room as Mahoney walked in and immediately began. "Okay everyone, please sit and quiet down," he bellowed out as he reached the front of the room.

He turned to face everyone and continued. "As you may have noticed, I have called everyone here, except for Jonas. It has become apparent to me that something has happened involving one of our members in captivity, and that it may have a profound effect on him if he were to find out. So, that's why I've called you all here without him. I need to inform each of you of what has taken place."

He paused. "There has been another development, and another video posted on the internet."

Murmurs swept across the silent room, and everyone glanced around and back to Mahoney as he continued. "The video does show one of our group tied and kneeling. That member was not beheaded or killed that we know of at this point.

"However, the terrorist issued a stern warning to the United States as to what will happen if their demands are not met." He began to pace across the room. "The member shown in the video was Cayce." Another round of murmurs filled the room.

"Now, I do have the video, but I feel it would not be beneficial at this point to show it. I will, however, tell each of you that she has been beaten, her head has been shaved, and she wears rags for clothing." He stated, fighting to keep his emotions in check before continuing.

"What I need from each of you at the present is to help keep an eye on Jonas. If he finds out about Cayce, he will go rogue. We have learned he is prone to doing this."

Once again, he paused before continuing. "So, what I need from you is this: keep close watch over him and keep me informed if you think he is acting suspicious. Please keep this information to yourselves. I will tell Jonas about it when the time is right, and not before then. Now, any questions?" He concluded.

The room was silent, and everyone's faces showed concern, not only for Cayce, but also Jonas. The silence was broken when the two double doors flew open at the rear of the room and there stood Jonas.

An uneasy silence filled the room. Unconcernedly, Mahoney began to play it off as Jonas being late to the meeting. "So, the prodigal son does show. Where've you been? We've been waiting on you."

Jonas glanced around the room and back to Mahoney. "I guess I missed the memo." He shrugged his shoulders and entered the room. The room broke into a quick burst of nervous laughter and died off just as quickly.

"Well, have a seat and we'll get started," Mahoney commented as he motioned towards a chair. He began to lay out the plans and what to expect once they arrived in Iraq.

An hour later, he finished. "Everyone finish up with the packing. We need to leave here in one hour. We have a flight to catch."

An hour later, they all loaded up into a couple of vans Mahoney had leased, and made their way to the airfield. Within fifteen minutes, they were in the air and Mahoney was motioning for everyone to come to the back of the cabin.

Once everyone was situated, he began speaking in a low voice. "I have received more information," he began and paused while glancing towards the front of the cabin. "Our source has decided it is best we not count on the United States to send out a rescue mission. Whatever the reason, I'm not sure."

He paused and glanced over the group once again to make sure no one was headed their way or listening. "He has hired a mercenary group to help us complete the mission and get our people out of there. This group will meet with us in Rafha once we arrive."

He paused again and looked over the group. "This group is already here - here meaning the Middle East - and are currently in route. So, once we arrive in Rafha we wait for them.

"Mica, Tori, and I will remain in Rafha coordinating once me meet up with them and get underway." Tori was a telepath with minor abilities in telekinesis and Mica was a handler. "That's it for now. Go, sit back, and relax. It's going to be a very long day."

Jeff returned to his seat. Jonas sat beside him and sighed. He sat for a minute in thought, then turned to Jeff. "Why would the source hire a mercenary group at this point? I mean we have seven days before our time runs out; why the rush now? Has something else happened?"

Jeff nervously sat contemplating as the corner of his right eye began to twitch as it does when he's nervous. After working up his nerve, he responded. "I think Mahoney would tell us if anything has happened. I wouldn't read too much into it at this point. Best we just wait it out and see what happens from here."

Jonas nodded, but noticed the eye twitch and knew Jeff was hiding something. "If you say so, but something is very fishy here. I'm not sure what, but something's not right."

The aircraft touched down in Kuwait City at 1615 hours, and after disembarking, Mahoney was once again on the phone. After a few minutes, he hung up and addressed the group. "Follow me; our ride is here." Through another contact, he had arranged a ride to Rafha.

The group followed him through the terminal and out the front doors. Waiting outside was an old farming truck full of vegetables for the market. "Well, it's not a limo, but I guess it beats walking, I suppose?" Jonas piped up in a smartass tone, which amused everyone - everyone except Mahoney.

An hour and five minutes later, moving at a crawling speed, they arrived in Rafha. It was 1805 hours, and they had twenty-five minutes before they were to meet their guide Aljeb.

"Okay, I want everyone stay around this area until I return. I'm going to meet our guide." Mahoney turned north and headed through the town. They were standing in an old rundown market square, looking like a bunch of tourists, glancing around not knowing exactly what to do.

Slowly they began to split up and walk away from each other. The vendors yelled out to them in Arabic, trying to persuade them to buy their goods as they walked around window-shopping.

Fifteen minutes after Mahoney had left, Jonas was standing next to an Arabic woman in front of a produce stand. Out of the blue, the woman turned and spoke to Jonas with a thick and very masculine Arabic accent. "You are one of the Americans. Yes?"

Caught by surprise, Jonas stood there stunned for a few seconds, not because of the question, but because it was a man's voice. After a moment of recovery, he irrevocably replied, "Who's asking, and why are you dressed as a woman?"

The man lowered his veil and revealed his face. "It's me, Aljeb," he replied pulling the veil back in place. "I disguise myself so no one recognizes me. I could be put to death, as well as my family, if I am found to be helping you."

Jonas nodded and smiled as he looked over this man in drag, and with a touch of sarcasm in his voice stated, "I gotta say, you make a fine-looking woman."

He fought back the urge to laugh. "Why aren't you at the rendezvous point instead of here?" he added after a moment of recovery.

Aljeb glanced at Jonas and quickly back to the produce, picking up a fresh melon and smelling it. "I feel it is best to select where we meet at random. It makes it harder for someone to follow or overhear."

He scanned around to make sure no one was around them. After a moment of silence, he continued. "People I have worked for in the past have called me the chameleon, for the way I blend in to a situation."

Jonas smugly retorted, "Fitting. So, I guess we just wait here until Mahoney returns. I don't expect he will wait too long for you to show before he heads back."

Aljeb continued to act as if he were shopping. "Just go about sightseeing as you were. I'll be around watching until he shows." Jonas nodded, and they split off in different directions.

Twenty minutes later, Mahoney returned not looking too happy. Jonas approached him and spent the next five minutes explaining what had transpired after his departure. After pointing out the female figure across the square, Mahoney began making his way there, acting like a shopper.

Aljeb noticed Mahoney when he returned and began to make his way towards him, doing the same. Eventually, the two found themselves at the same rug vendor stand.

"You are Mahoney. Yes?" A man's voice whispered.

Mahoney pretended not to hear, and after a few seconds he replied, "Yes, I am Mahoney."

"Good, good…meet in ten minutes at the end of the street to your left," the man in drag replied, then very nonchalantly turned and left.

Mahoney stayed at the rug stand for another minute, then turned and walked back to Jonas. "Get everyone together and have them meet me here ASAP." Jonas nodded and hurried to gather everyone.

Eight minutes later, they were at the designated end of the street. The area was deserted; not a sign of life was in sight. They waited. Ten minutes passed and no Aljeb. Mahoney was about to call an audible and head back to the airstrip when the high-pitched sound of an unoiled door hinge rang out.

A small dark-skinned man stood peering out of the door of a small shanty. "Come quickly," he said, motioning for them to come. Mahoney, Jonas, and the rest of the group quickly walked to the door and entered.

Once inside, the man closed the door and turned. "I am Aljeb, better known by most as the chameleon," he stated as he walked to the small window and peered out.

Mahoney reached out and shook the man's hand. "I as you know am Mahoney. Jonas you've met, and this is the rest of my team." He introduced the rest of the group one by one.

"Very good to meet all of you," Aljeb declared. "This will be your place for as long as you need it to work. It once belonged to my brother-in-law who is now deceased. I must warn you though, do not go outside. If you are spotted, it will only bring big trouble."

He paused again, peering out the window. "I will bring you food, supplies, and whatever else you may need. Just tell me what you wish and I will bring it, okay?"

"As of right now we need to get unpacked and ready to go. When can you be ready?" Mahoney asked.

Aljeb began shaking his head excitedly. "No, no. We must wait until nightfall. It is far too dangerous to go now while the sun is still shining."

Mahoney exhaled a deep breath of frustration but understood. "Alright, when can we leave?"

"We may go in two hours, but before then I will bring food. We have much to discuss before we go," Aljeb replied and turned towards the door.

"Very well, in two hours we leave," Mahoney reluctantly acknowledged.

Aljeb nodded. "I will return shortly. Stay inside and out of sight." He cracked the door open and peered out to see if it was clear and left.

"Okay people," Mahoney announced, "you heard the man. Let's get unpacked and ready. We have two hours; use the time wisely."

Jonas had reservations about entering into a known terrorist state unarmed. He wondered if they were to get any weapons at all before or after entering

Iraq. After he unpacked and sorted his equipment, he headed to Mahoney to find out.

Keeping his voice low, he questioned Mahoney. "Sir, are we to assume that we are going into Iraq unarmed? If so, will we be issued any weapons after we enter?"

Mahoney stopped what he was doing and smiled before replying. "I was wondering if anyone was going to ask me that." The smile on his face grew, and Jonas became even more confused over this reaction.

Mahoney turned and announced, "Can I have everyone over here for a minute, and please bring your cases." Everyone grabbed their cases.

After giving time for everyone to get situated, Mahoney continued. "Jonas has brought up a good question: he wanted to know if you were going to be issued any weapons either before or after entering Iraq. I had been waiting for that question. Each of you, please set your cases flat on the floor as if you are going to open them."

Each case was placed on the floor. "Good!" Mahoney continued. "Now take the key and place it into the locks. Turn the key right until the locks release."

There was a simultaneous sound of locks releasing as Mahoney continued. "Open the case and examine it thoroughly. Tell me if you see anything."

Each of the group examined the cases. No one noticed anything strange or wrong. No one except Jonas. He noticed the bottom half of the cases appeared to be slightly deeper than it was showing inside. He decided to keep quiet to see if he was right.

Mahoney, now basking in the glory that no one had noticed anything, began once again. "Now, if you will please turn the key back to the center position as if you were going to remove the key." Everyone did so.

"Everyone there yet?" Mahoney asked. "Okay, now turn the key left." As they did, another resounding click was heard from each case and the inside of the case popped up about one half inch. "Go ahead lift it out," Mahoney instructed.

Jonas lifted the tray out of the case, and beneath it he found his .45 and three 9 mil hand guns along with several clips of ammo. "Pretty cool, huh?" Mahoney boasted with a large smile. "So, Jonas to answer your question, no you will not go unarmed." Jonas was content knowing he would be going in armed, so he went back to finish getting ready to go.

Aljeb returned with food and clothing. "The clothing is so no one will recognize you as Americans," he stated as he tossed the clothing on the small table. "Please eat. I will return in twenty minutes and then we will talk," he added.

Twenty minutes later, Aljeb returned with two men in tow. Everyone in the little house freaked and scrambled for their weapons when Aljeb walked in. Aljeb instantly raised his hands and screamed, *"No! No! They are your men!"*

"What do you mean they are our men?" Jonas replied. "We don't know them."

A tall, muscular black man walked forward. "Uncle Davy sent us." It was the mercenary group that was hired to help. Mahoney ordered everyone to lower their weapons and turned to Aljeb. "Why didn't you warn us that you went to get them and bring them here? Someone could have gotten hurt or killed."

The man once again began to speak. "Sorry sir, but that would be my fault. I insisted that my second and I come here personally to go over what plans you had, and see if we could assist in any way. We could have waited outside until he could warn you, but it would have increased the chances of us being seen."

Mahoney thought on this. "Point taken, and we're sure glad to see you guys. I'm Kyle Mahoney," he stated as he reached out to shake hands.

"Captain John Henry Bates, and my second Captain Jerry Franks." He replied as he took Mahoney's hand to shake it. "Time is running short sir. We best go over what plans you've got."

The southern drawl in the captain's voice was thick and sweet. Jonas guessed it was from Alabama or Georgia, but whichever it was, being a southern boy himself, it was music to his ears.

Franks was a short stocky man with rather small ears and a comical face. Although, his demeanor was anything but comical, which Jonas had realized when he jokingly asked, "So…how's Mrs. Shrek?" which at the time seemed funny, but afterwards he decided this was not a good move on his part.

Franks shot him a look and sternly retorted, "Are you calling my wife a troll?"

Jonas froze and swallowed hard, thinking Franks took him seriously. A full minute had passed before

Franks smiled, "I'm fucking with you man. I'm not married."

Jonas drew a breath of relief. "Thank God…I thought for a second I was dead meat." They both laughed as Franks slapped him on the shoulder, and they joined the others.

VI: Confrontations

The black sheik and a handful of men planned to leave sometime within the next few days to head north closer to a battle in the city of Al Bukamal in Syria.

Al Bukamal would be the first city in Syria taken in his quest to control the Middle East, and he wanted to be there when it happened. Along the way, he would stop at the training camp in Al-Kasrah.

The sheik summoned what he considered to be his top three enforcers into the small room that was his office. "I wish to take the female with me when I head north in a few days. I think the men in battle would appreciate the fresh companionship, but before I do, I wish her to be brought to me. I want to taste her flesh before anyone else, and once I am finished with her, you may have her until the morning."

The enforcers left the room to retrieve Cayce, who was lying on her side in the middle of the floor, still trying to find a way to free her hands. The psychic guard was peering out the window when the door flew open.

The same three men that had been there several times before walked into the room. Cayce knew this was not going to be good. So far, each time they came back to her, the beatings got worse and worse. She sat upright and tried her best to scoot away from them.

The shorter man with the blue eyes said something in Arabic to the guard, who turned and left the room. The other two men grabbed her by the arms and lifted her to a standing position. Her arms were sore and tired from being tied behind her all this time, and she squealed in pain.

The shorter man approached her. "It is time for you to become our servant." He smiled. "For now you belong to the sheik, but soon after you will be mine and theirs," as he denoted the men standing with him.

Cayce's eyes widened, and she screamed, *"No! You bastard...no!"* The man slapped her hard across the side of her face and she went limp. They took her to the sheik, sat her into a chair, and shook her until she awoke.

She sat dazed, not sure where she was or why. Realizing what had happened, she began to scream again. *"You son of a bi-"* Another resounding slap echoed the room as the shorter man hit her from behind, and once again she went lifeless.

She awoke a short time later and found she was naked, gagged and tied spread eagle to each of the four bed posts. The sheik was mounting her and thrusting himself into her as he looked down upon her and smiled. "You will get used to this, for this will be your calling from now on my sweet." He began to laugh aloud as he plunged onward.

Cayce began to weep, silently at first and growing into a wail. She silently prayed that if this was her fate that God would end it. When the sheik had finished, she lay motionless, and as he left the room, the shorter man entered and began to undress. Once again, she began to cry.

After their meeting, they loaded up and got ready to leave. Jeff went into a daze and began getting a vision. Jonas noticed and went to yell for Mahoney, but before he got the words out of his mouth, the entire psychic group also started having a vision, all at the same time.

Bates and Franks stood and watched in amazement as it took place. Bates was officially spooked, and as he and Franks unconsciously backed up a step or two, he yelled out, "What kind of voodoo shit is this?"

"They're psychics, and they're having a vision!" Jonas retorted.

"All of them at once? This is some scary shit," Bates countered, while backing up.

After a matter of minutes, each of the psychics came out of their vision, each with a nervous look on their face, glancing between Jonas and Mahoney. Jonas could feel that something had just happened, something very bad.

"Okay," Jonas began. "What's with all the concerned looks? Someone please tell me what just happened, and don't fucking lie to me."

"Hold on just a minute Jonas. Let's not get carried away or jump to conclusions until we've heard what this was all about," Mahoney intervened.

Jonas had suspected that things had been happening beyond his knowledge. He exploded in anger. *"No! You* hold on! It seems to me that from the start, certain members of this group - or the whole fucking team for all I know - have been keeping something from me. Now either you fess up, or I'll go and find out for myself."

Jonas got into Mahoney's face. Mahoney could feel the anger boiling out of him. There was total silence in the room as Jonas looked around the room and back to Mahoney. *"Well?"*

Mahoney felt he had no choice; he would tell Jonas everything and hope he did not short circuit in the process. "Alright, you're right. I haven't been forthcoming with you," he stated, "but I felt keeping it from you was for your own benefit as well as for the mission, and not because of any other reason."

Jonas studied Mahoney as he finished his sentence and intervened. "It's Cayce isn't it?" The look on Mahoney's face said it all. "What's happened to her? Is she dead?" he asked, his voice beginning to waver.

"No, no! She's not dead. Still, if we don't locate and get to her soon, she and the others may as well be, or wish they were," Mahoney replied.

"Tell me what's happened and don't skip or sweeten any part of it on my account," Jonas retorted as anger and fear built within him.

"Okay, I'll tell you everything I know at this point, but first let me find out what has happened so I can give you the whole story." Mahoney motioned for Jeff and the other psychics to follow him outside where they could talk in private.

Jonas waited, pacing back and forth in the room like a caged wild animal. Occasionally, he would mumble something to himself and his arms would flail around in frustration.

Bates and Franks watched and whispered to one another about what had transpired. "Have you ever seen anything like this in the past?" Franks asked Bates.

Bates shook his head in astonishment and leaned towards Franks. "No, I haven't, but I've read books where shit like this had taken place, and I gotta admit, it's a helluva lot more freaky seeing it in person than reading about it."

After a matter of minutes, Mahoney and the others returned, and Mahoney tentatively approached Jonas. "You sure you want to know all the details?"

Jonas shot him a look. Without further hesitation he replied, "You're damn right I do. If something has happened to Cayce, I want to know. If someone is going to die over this, I want to know what they did and who they are."

Mahoney slightly nodded his head, "Okay, come on over here. I have something I need you to see." Jonas followed him to the small table where the laptop was sitting. Mahoney opened it and began typing in passwords. After a moment, the file came up, and he clicked on it. "This was broadcast over the internet yesterday," he stated.

Jonas sat and watched in silence as it played. When it ended, he sat rubbing his temples as he fought to keep his emotions in check. He suddenly swept his arms across the table sending the laptop and everything else on it across the room and onto the floor, losing the battle.

He abruptly turned to face Mahoney and bellowed out, "There will be no holding back. There will be no remorse and there will be no hesitation. They will die and they will die by my hands, this much I promise. I'm warning you now, don't try to stop me. I will not – I repeat *not* - allow them make a sex slave out of her. I will see them in hell first." The rage and the fire in his eyes were flaring to the point; one could almost see actual flames.

Mahoney took a deep breath. "That's not all I'm afraid," hesitating to continue. "The latest vision, the one they just had, it… Well they…"

"Spit it out!" Jonas yelled cutting him off, growing more and more frustrated.

"They've raped her Jonas." Mahoney finally blurted out. "I'm sorry, but there's no other way to say it."

The weight of the world hit Jonas head-on and sent him reeling. The final straw had been drawn and there was no putting it back. He had reached his limit and was out of control of sanity itself. *"No! God, no!"* he yelled as he grabbed anything within his reach and flung it across the room.

Everyone in the room ducked down and clasped their hands to their ears as his voice echoed and amplified in the tiny room. He had a crazed, uncontrolled look in his eyes. His face was beet red and his teeth were clenched.

Jeff attempted to grab Jonas and calm him down, but Jonas instinctively turned on him. Before Jeff could respond, Jonas hit him with a deadly glare that sent pain into his mind. Instantly he fell to the floor in agonizing pain as Jonas turned back to Mahoney, and everything went black.

Jeff's effort to console Jonas had given Mahoney enough time to get his bearings, and using a mag light, he had knocked Jonas unconscious. Jonas now lay motionless on the floor.

"Is everyone okay?" Mahoney asked glancing around the room. Luckily, no one was seriously hurt, except for maybe Jeff, who was still on the floor holding his head. Mahoney quickly went and knelt down beside him. "Jeff! Jeff! Are you alright?" he questioned as he vigorously shook him.

"Ouch! Son of a bitch that hurt!" Jeff exclaimed as he started to come to. "What the hell happened?" He slipped back down onto his rump when he tried to stand.

"Jonas happened, and you're damn lucky. It might have been a lot worse," Mahoney stated. Bates and Franks approached Mahoney and Jeff, as Jeff finally got back to his feet.

"That's the damnedest thing I ever saw in my life," Bates said in amazement. "What in the hell did I just witness? How did he do what he just did? Can he control it or does it just happen?" He hurled question after question.

"Yes, at will, and a lot worse than you just saw. He is one deadly individual to be around when he's pissed," Mahoney stated. "Come on, let's get him off the floor and see if we can wake him."

Thirty minutes later, Jonas sat stone-faced and angry. Mahoney approached him and knelt down beside him, and that is when he noticed something different about his look.

There were two small white patches of hair at each of his temples, about the size of a dime. He was certain that they had not been there before and wondered if it had to do with his gift. He disregarded it for the time being and turned to Jonas.

Jonas remained stone-faced and glared back at Mahoney. "Jonas, I'm sorry that I kept this information from you, but I knew it would have a profound effect on you. I can't have you going rogue on me right now. This team and I need you, and we need you to be mission-oriented. I decided to give you this information in the hopes that I could still rely on you. So tell me…can I?"

Jonas, still glaring, sat quietly for a few more seconds. "You can, but only until we find our people. After that, it's either work with me, or I go it alone. The only retribution the terrorist may have from me is if they put a bullet in me first."

Mahoney nodded in understanding. "Okay, I'm going to hold you to that." He got back to his feet and announced, "Alright everyone, finish packing and be ready to leave in thirty."

He turned to Bates and Franks. "Under the circumstances, a reassessment of our plans seems to be in order." They both agreed and the three of them headed for the corner of the room away from everyone else. Aljeb followed.

Bates, still in utter shock began speaking first. "I take it that what we saw was his psychic ability; am I correct?"

Mahoney nodded, "One of several abilities he possesses, and also the most deadly. Jonas is a "one-in-a-million," in the sense that not only is he a remote viewer in two ways, but he can also, as you have just observed, inflict pain. He can also invoke the power of suggestion."

"Hmm…that could be very useful," Bates remarked as he glanced at Franks. "Can he control it? I mean can he do it at will?"

"Oh, yes. What you saw is what happens when he loses it though. You see, if the endorphins released in his brain amass to where it's too much, he goes haywire and loses control over what happens. He somewhat short circuits. It's why I choose not to give him certain information that I think could cause him to overload, so to speak."

"And…this woman in the video is someone special to him I take it?" Bates questioned.

"Yes, she is the one and only love interest in his life. She pretty much brought him back from the brink. Unfortunately, they've been apart for a little time now, and it's the first time he has seen her in months. I was afraid something like this would happen if he was made aware of her situation or saw the video, and I was right."

"It was the strangest thing I have ever seen," Aljeb stated shaking his head in wonder. "I mean, it scared the bejeebers out of me," he added.

"With the situation being what it is," Mahoney began again, "plans need to be revised. So this is what

I'm thinking: you may add to or bring up questions or suggestions at any time." Mahoney laid out his new plans with the other three adding in their suggestions, and before long, a new plan was formulated.

"Can I get everyone over her please?" Mahoney announced, and after everyone had gathered, he continued. "With the advice of Capt. Bates, Lt. Franks, and Aljeb, we have come up with a new plan that we feel will work. We will split into three teams. Team one will consist of the following people: Jeff, Robert, Gill, and Lt. Franks. Franks and Jeff will share command responsibilities."

Jeff and Robert were both psychics, and Gill was a telepath, each with prior military experience and all with a vast amount of knowledge and experience in what they were doing.

"Team two will consist of Jonas, Walt, Marcy, and Aljeb along with Capt. Bates and his team," Mahoney continued. "Capt. Bates and Jonas will share command responsibilities."

Walt, a prior Green Beret and psychic for team two, was medically discharged after his chute became entangled during a jump and took a hard landing. He was lucky to survive the fall.

Marcy was prior medical and the telepath. She was also the only female heading into the field, mainly because she was trained in battlefield medicine. She had also served in 'Desert Storm' where she earned the Purple Heart. She knew how to handle herself.

"Finally, team three will be consist of myself, Mica, Tori, and Jason. We will set up and coordinate operations from here."

Mica was fairly new to Stargate having only been there for nine months before it ended. She had minor abilities in telekinesis and acted as a handler.

Tori was the telepath of the group. She also had not been with Stargate very long before it was disbanded.

Jason was the psychic and had been with Stargate only a little while longer than Mica.

"Each group will have a handheld radio system such as this one." Mahoney held up a rather large handheld radio. "I will now let Lt. Franks explain the system."

Franks moved to the center of the group and began. "This radio system is not your run of the mill system. It is undeniably the most secure and advanced system operating in the world today. It works off several thousands of frequencies, modulated in a matter of one millisecond to send and receive messages.

"It has its own set of satellites from which it transmits these messages. Each satellite scrambles and retransmits the signal again in thousands of separate frequencies to other separate satellites before it transmits each signal back to the earth, where the intended radio, such as this one, puts the message back into proper format.

"This system is not being used by our military or by anyone else in the world yet. It was designed and built by Honeywell for one reason only, and that reason was that the former sitting president requested it.

"You will only be able to contact a base station and each other. The base will, of course, be here with Col. Mahoney as well as one other at a non-disclosed location. Other than that, it's a closed system. Each handheld operates just as a normal handheld does. Except for the fact that it's a little larger, it looks the same.

"Do not - and I mean under any circumstance - let these units fall into the wrong hands. Am I clear on that?" Everyone nodded. "Good! One last thing: this radio has a built in GPS, and from the base alone, it can locate you or any other handheld of its configuration within a few feet. Now, if you have no other questions, that's all I have." The room remained silent. "Good. Back to you, sir."

Mahoney replaced Franks in the middle of the group and finished off the meeting. "Get yourselves ready; you leave in ten." The group dispersed to finish packing their gear.

As the plan was drawn up, team one would head west of town to a GPS point approximately 162 kilometers. Team two would head east to a GPS point approximately 80.5 kilometers.

Upon arriving at these coordinates, team one would head north to the next GPS point at 162.5 kilometers and team two would turn north to the next GPS setting for another 80 kilometers.

The mission was timed in such a way as to have both groups reach their destinations at relatively the same time. This would be done by team one making the journey completely by automobile.

Team two would make only the first leg of the trip and a small part of the second leg by automobile, and complete the rest of the second stage by foot. Each team would contact team three for further instructions upon arrival at each point.

The teams loaded up and headed for the first set of coordinates.

VII: Wasteland

The first leg of the trip was a quiet one for Jonas and his team. Still raging from the information he had received the thought of those dirty bastards manhandling Cayce, along with what they had done to her, it was too much for him to handle, and he needed an outlet.

He felt that once the group turned north and headed for the second set of coordinates, it could be safe enough to try to trip to Cayce. The only catch was that in order for him to trip to see around her, he would first need to trip into her. Only then could he make the jump out and into the area she was being kept.

They would soon arrive at the first set of coordinates and Bates would make the call back to team three. After that, it was a short ride across the border and on foot from there. Jonas was growing more impatient with the whole process.

The thought of jumping ship had crossed his mind several times since they had boarded the truck, but he had given his word and he would at least wait until he had them located.

The border between Saudi and Syria was patrolled constantly on both sides. Aljeb had scouted the border and found the two most likely places to cross without being detected. At these points, a patrol would come by every fifteen minutes like clockwork.

"We must time our crossing so that we go as soon as they are out of sight," Aljeb stated with a sharp Arabic accent. "We go too soon or too late, we will be seen and that will not be a good thing. I will go ahead and see if it's clear once we arrive, and I will signal when it's clear to go. Okay?"

Bates was uncertain what exactly to think of Aljeb. He apparently was a fair guide, but his phrases threw him for a loop at times. He had worked with many Middle Eastern guides and Aljeb admittedly was the first he felt was truly missing an oar in his boat.

They were minutes away from the first set of coordinates. Jonas sat quietly listening to a conversation that Walt and Marcy were having when something Walt said caught his attention. "Excuse me, Walt. Did I just hear you say it seems that whatever they are using to block us drops away during the times you receive a vision?" he asked.

Walt, looking confused, replied cautiously. "Well…yes, it seems so. Why?"

Jonas was getting a little excited and kept digging. "So what you're saying is there's an opening in the block during the times you receive a vision… correct?"

Walt nodded his head bemused. "Yes, I believe so."

This gave Jonas a thought: if he could trip into Cayce or Doc or any one of the other members during that time, then…

He turned back to Walt and in a hushed tone asked, "Can you tell beforehand when you're about to have a vision?"

Walt was starting to get the picture and replied, "Sure sometimes, but you're not going to try what I think you are…are you?"

Jonas' mind was racing as he slowly nodded his head. "Just let me know if you think you're about to get a vision, and if possible who it's from. I'll take it from there, alright?"

Walt and Marcy both looked at each other and back to Jonas. "Are you sure about this?" Marcy finally stated, more out of concern than anything else.

Jonas, out of frustration snapped back. "Look, if I can locate them, it would save a lot of time and effort for both teams, because someone - us, them, or both - is headed in the wrong direction. So, are you helping me or not?"

Walt and Marcy glanced at each other again. Marcy nodded ever so slightly to Walt who turned back and faced Jonas. "Okay, you've got our help, and I'll try to give you as much information as I can before and during the vision."

Jonas reached out his hand. "Thank you!"

Moments later, they arrived at the first set of coordinates. Aljeb jumped out of the back of the truck and ran off to the north, and a few of the mercenaries jumped out to set up perimeter guards.

Bates got out of the front cab with the handheld radio. He spoke into it as he walked off in front of the truck. "Team two. Team three." Before the reply came, he was out of hearing distance.

Jonas turned to Walt and Marcy. "Here's what I need you to do. First, Walt let me know you're about to get a vision. I will wait to see if you can tell whom you're connected to. If - and only if - you can tell me who it's from, I will begin to trip into them.

"With any luck, we will be close enough that I can trip in and back out to get an overhead view. Marcy, if I'm not close by. I need you to get any information Walt may have to me wherever I am, and then stand guard. If anyone notices or get close, whisper into my ear to warn me. I'll still be tripping, but I'll be able to hear you. Okay?"

They both nodded their acceptance. "I sure hope you've given thought to the repercussions if this goes sour and gets someone killed," Walt stated out of concern.

Jonas shot him a concerned yet understanding look. "Yeah, it has crossed my mind, and I hope it doesn't come to that."

Eventually, Bates walked back to the truck and around to where Jonas and the others were sitting. "Well, as soon as Aljeb returns we cross the border and go about forty clicks. Then it's on foot from there."

Jonas nodded. "So from there on foot, we go another 12.5 miles to our final GPS point, correct?"

"Correct," Bates replied. "We'll need to maintain around 2.5 miles per hour to arrive on time."

"That's a pretty good pace in this sand. Are you sure we can do it?" Walt questioned.

Bates nodded as he responded, "Yes. Fortunately, from this point it's basically flat wasteland as far as the eye can see. We will also have to contend with the sand, but we should make good time crossing it, barring we don't run into trouble along the way. There will be dunes as we get closer, but it shouldn't slow us down too much."

Ten minutes later, Aljeb reappeared from the darkness. "Alright, we are ready to move closer. The patrols have gone by and will be coming back soon, and after they pass again, we will cross. Chop-chop. Let's go!"

Bates shook his head. "That man has got a way with words," he exclaimed, smiling as he went back to the cab of the truck. Thirteen minutes later the patrols passed again, and they proceeded across the border. They traveled another twenty minutes, and the trucks stopped and they unloaded.

Jeff, along with Franks and team one, had yet to arrive at their first set of designated coordinates. They had further to go, but they would make better time across the border.

Jeff was still feeling the effects of Jonas and his special ability. It had left a frightening feeling within his soul and he could not shake it. He tried to explain to himself exactly what it felt like, the closest thing he could compare it to be, was being shocked by electricity, and a lot of it.

After the teams had departed, Mahoney spoke to President Davy and found that the facial scan revealed no matches. The man in black was clever; he had made sure he covered most of his face and what was not covered he applied black makeup to, especially around his exposed eyes. This effect made him nearly impossible to identify.

Mahoney updated Davy on their current situation. Davy informed them he would be monitoring on his base system, which he had installed in his home, and wished them all luck.

"Please, if you can, save her." He ended the call by saying he would be in touch.

Mahoney had a gut feeling the mission was not going to be easy. Wherever they were keeping the hostages, he was sure they were going to be ready for anything. He silently hoped that the small 28-man group split into two teams could do the job.

Air support would have been nice, but without it, he was sure there would be losses. The acceptable loss equation factored into their hopes for success. Losing too many would jeopardize the whole mission. He also felt that loss of life was never good, no matter the reward.

Team three was on pins and needles. From there, they would have time to kill as both teams had reached point one, and were in route to point two. This would take each team approximately two to two-and-a-half hours if nothing went wrong.

Mahoney decided to start going back over the files on the Brotherhood. He needed a name to go with the man in black. Who was he? Where did he come from?

An hour into the ride to the second set of coordinates, Jeff sat in the back of the farm truck in deep thought. Somewhere in the back of his mind, he still had a nagging feeling about the first time he connected with Cayce. There was something there; he was not sure what it was, but it had an oddly obvious familiarity to it, like he should know it or had felt it previously.

He did not think it was the connection to Cayce, but it felt like a connection - a connection to someone he had connected with once before. He just could not figure out whom.

He had never connected to Cayce before that time, nor Doc or any of the other members of the team being held as far as he could remember. The thought of it being someone within the Brotherhood came to mind, but he could not imagine who in the Brotherhood that was alive that he could have connected to at any given time.

Oman was the only one he could think of at first, but he suddenly thought of someone else: the man in black. He called himself The Black Sheik, and the name sheik rang a bell. Leon Pasqual Kerchief, alias Ali Mohammad Kerchief, alias The Sheik, and now The Black Sheik. Jeff would bet his life on it.

Kerchief was a French foreign national turned radical terrorist and upon accepting the Muslim ways.

He changed his name to Ali Mohammad Kerchief, keeping his last name mostly due to his vanity.

In later years he was dubbed 'The Sheik' by the CIA and the name stuck. Now appears he has changed it again and with this change also came his true colors in terms of terrorism. He was now the new and ruthless leader of the Brotherhood.

He had to get word to Mahoney immediately. Banging on the roof of the truck, the driver finally stopped and Franks jumped out and quickly went to the back where Jeff met him.

Jeff quickly explained the epiphany he had, and said he needed to contact Mahoney ASAP. Franks pulled out the radio and called team three. Miles away, Bates was walking along with his team members in team two, when the conversation came over their radio.

Jonas walked beside Bates, stopping dead in his tracks as everyone gathered around. Over the next five minutes, they listened as Jeff explained to Mahoney what he surmised.

Damn it! I'll bet my ass Jonas and the rest of the team are listening to this whole conversation,

Mahoney thought to himself, and he could not have been more right.

Overall, this had a negative effect on Jonas. After hearing Kerchief's name, he turned and walked away from the team. Bates noticed and followed him. "What's wrong Jonas?" he asked as he approached him. Jonas stood gazing out over the wasteland. Bates waited, and after getting no response, he called his name again.

Eventually, Jonas turned to him. "Kerchief was the one that got away from us last year when Dallas blew himself up and put me in the hospital." He looked down at the dirt. "It all makes sense now, why our people and why me. *Damn, I wanted that son of a bitch!* We should have had him then, and if not for Dallas, we would have."

Bates began to develop a little understanding of what Jonas was saying. He stepped towards Jonas as if to say something and stopped when Jonas began to speak again.

Jonas began kicking and shuffling the sand around beneath his feet. "Dallas wasn't a bad kid, confused maybe, but deep down a good kid. It really sucked to see him go the way he did, although I think he deserved it. I just don't understand how those bastards do it. How do they take a smart kid and brainwash him in the way they did? How do these kids let themselves be taken in like this? I mean to turn on your country, your family, everything you were raised to believe? How? How do they do it?"

Bates found himself at a loss for words on that topic. After a few seconds, he approached Jonas, put his hand on his shoulder, and tried to elaborate. "Impressionable minds are easy to persuade, especially when they're told of the false rewards a new life that religion can offer them.

"Most of the young people they persuade are susceptible because their home life and life in general stinks. They're looking for a better way, and these groups of terrorist offer them that. Even though false in their claims, the young people buy into it."

Bates walked around to face Jonas and continued. "Tell me more about this Kerchief guy. Why was he in the United States?"

Jonas gave a look as if exploring his memory, and then it suddenly came to him. *"Oh Shit!"* flew out of his mouth before he realized what he was saying. "I wonder if Mahoney recalled the reason. Let's go; we need to contact him now!" He dashed back to the area where everyone else was waiting and demanded the radio.

"Team two, team three." Jonas articulated into the radio and after a team few seconds three responded. "Team three, team two."

"Are you alright Jo?" Mahoney responded having known that they had heard the conversation between Jeff and himself. He was expecting Jonas to call after hearing, and he was not sure how he was taking it.

"Do you remember why he was in the United States?" In his haste, Jonas forgot to press the call button.

Mahoney had only gotten part of what Jonas was asking. "He was in the United States?" was the entire message he received. He thought Jonas had remembered everything about Kerchief and the airport, and then - *"Fucking sleepers. Damn!"* He burst out as the realization struck him.

Mica, Tori, and Jason were startled by this sudden outburst. Mahoney grabbed the mic and responded to Jonas. "Team two, I'll call you right back." He took out his cell and dialed the number for the former president.

Having overheard the conversation, Davy contacted Bill Winters, director of the FBI. Davy answered within half a ring. "Hold on, I'll put us on conference call."

After a second or two he continued. "Colonel Mahoney, I have Bill Winters on the call with us and I have informed him of our situation. Bill, what can you tell us about these sleepers?"

Bill Winters had formed a task force to track down the sleepers a year ago, when Oman had them infiltrate the United States with Kerchief. Even though he and his team had worked diligently, he had no idea how many they had captured, if any.

"Well sir, we have tracked down several members of the Brotherhood, including those we have only suspected. Not knowing exactly how many were sent over here, I have no way of knowing if we got them all. That being said, we are still relentless in our search," Bill responded.

When Kerchief fled the United States after the death of Oman, he had left behind suicide bombers spread all over the United States. These bombers, turned sleepers by Kerchief, were still there. A few had been located, and deported or jailed, but a lot more were still active and waiting.

"I see. I know it's no longer my place to tell you this Bill, but you need to sound the alarm and tell the President and higher-ups of what's taking place," Davy exclaimed. "While you're at it, please inform the President that if he needs my input to please call me, and that I requested you to do so."

"Yes sir I will, and sorry I couldn't be of more help," Bill responded.

"You have done well Bill, and thank you," Davy declared, and the line went dead.

"Colonel Mahoney," Davy began again, "as I previously mentioned, it's no longer my place to give orders, only to recommend. I strongly recommend you rescue our people, and if in the process you come across Kerchief, take him out before he has the chance to use those sleepers. It's our only chance to avoid another catastrophe like last year."

Mahoney had been considering the implications as the former President had been speaking to Bill, and had drawn the same conclusion. "Yes sir, we will do our best, but to be honest, it would make things a lot easier if we had our country's support."

Davy cleared his throat. "I know what I'm asking will be difficult to say the least, and I'm proud to have had the privilege to have known each and every one on that team. Still, I cannot guarantee that the sitting president will get off his ass in time to be of any help to you. With that being said, I'm sorry to say that it's on your shoulders until we hear otherwise."

Mahoney figured as much and was planning accordingly. "Sir, it has been our honor to serve you. If not for you, we wouldn't have ever existed as a team. As for what the sitting president will do, it really doesn't matter. I plan to move ahead with this as if it were on us to make it happen anyways. We will do our best sir because we have the best," he replied.

"Agreed," responded Davy. "Good luck, I'll be listening." There was a resounding click as he hung up the phone.

Mahoney had to inform the teams that they had a primary and secondary mission. First, locate and free the hostages, and second, locate and eliminate Kerchief if possible.

He glanced around to Mica and Tori, who were pretending not to listen. "I suppose you heard? It seems the rules to the game have changed once again, and this time I'm not sure we can handle it. However, we may be all that's standing in the way of another plot on the United States. So along with locating our team members, we now need to locate and take out Kerchief."

Both Tori and Mica sat quietly, before Tori spoke up. "So what does that mean for us?"

Mahoney stopped his pacing. "Well for starters it looks as though we will be staying here longer than planned. It also means that there's a higher possibility of getting someone hurt or killed in the process. I realize we need to save our people and get Kerchief, but at what risk? I need to think on this awhile. I'll be right back." He headed for the door and went out.

He could not lose any of his team by forcing them to take on the added mission, for as much as it needed to happen, he would never force them into such a situation. This needed to be their choice.

VIII: Cayce's Mind

In a downward spiral, Cayce's mind had become numb to what was happening to her body. In a bid to save her sanity, she shut off her feelings and forced herself not to think about what was happening.

She shut off the outside world and secluded herself deep inside the furthest recesses of her mind. She had to shield off all feelings and emotions, or else lose her mind during this process.

The Sheik and his goons took their turns on her, and she had just begun to think that the whole ordeal was finished when the door opened again, and the shorter man once again began to undress.

But locked safely within the confines of her own mind Cayce felt nothing. She laid on her back showing no emotions, her eyes in a dead gaze into oblivion.

A short time later, the shorter man entered the Sheik's office. "She is broken," he stated as he approached the Sheik. "She just lies motionless staring into nothing. These Americans act so tough, and yet they break so easily," he added, amused.

The Sheik turned in his seat. "That is good, get her cleaned up and bring her to me. Once I confirm she is broken, we can remove the bindings and let her roam freely within the compound. Keep her earphones on her and her psychic guard nearby. If she is truly broken, she will not try to run. Nevertheless, keep a close watch on her as she may be feigning."

Jonas, Bates, and the rest of team two continued their march to the second set of coordinates. Thirty minutes had passed since Jonas had talked to Mahoney, and he was beginning to wonder what the hell was happening.

He felt that under the circumstances this new information would change the mission, although he was not sure just how at this point. His first priority was to rescue Cayce and the others. Anything after that would just have to wait, including payback for what they had done to Cayce.

Bates continued to question Jonas on what he knew of Kerchief, and was getting a pretty good picture of what they were up against. "This Kerchief, or Black Sheik, or whatever you call this dude - he sounds like he's all about self-preservation, and not much about his troops or religion. I think once we can find and instill the fear of God into him, he'll crack and make a run for it, and when he does, it will cause his troops to lose confidence in him. The whole terrorist group may begin to fall like dominos."

Jonas listened, considering what Bates had surmised, and it made sense to him, though running was not what he wanted Kerchief to do. He wanted him to stand and fight; he wanted to see the look in his eyes when his final moments were at hand, not running like the coward he knew he was.

At the current pace, they would arrive at the second set of coordinates in about an hour, and Jonas was hoping that sometime between before then, Walt would have another vision.

Impatience and anxiety were tearing him apart. He felt as if he should be running instead of the casual walk that was taking place. He had to fight the urge to speak up or start an all-out run, or both.

Suddenly, Mahoney's voice rang out over the radio. "Team three. Teams one and two."

The mercenary carrying the radio knelt down, leaning his AK-47 against his leg, and removed the radio from his belt. "Team two copies," he replied into the radio.

After a few seconds, "Team one copies," also came across.

Mahoney's voice came across the radio again. "Sorry it took so long to get back to you, but I need to ask everyone a question, and I need an answer ASAP. If anyone refuses, there will be no hard feelings. With that being said, and with the circumstances having changed, we've been tasked with an added mission. In addition to our primary mission, this will, without a doubt, increase the odds of putting each of you in harm's way, as well as keep you in theater longer than expected.

"Despite this, it's a necessary mission. Since we are already here, we may as well do it if we can. So, along with the mission to rescue or comrades, we also need to find and stop Kerchief if possible. Ordinarily, this would be outside our realm of responsibility, but Kerchief still has control of several sleepers within the United States. We're not exactly sure of how many there are.

"These sleepers are trained suicide bombers, and what remains of the failed attack, which we were a part of over a year ago. I'll allow you to talk this over for five minutes as a group, and then I will need an answer. Again, there will be no hard feelings towards anyone who decides not to go. That's all for now; you have five minutes."

Everyone in team two stood in silence until Bates finally spoke. "Okay, I guess we should go around and give an answer one by one. I'll start off and say yes." Each of the mercenaries, as well as Aljeb and Jonas, also agreed. Walt and Marcy took a little longer to decide. Eventually Walt agreed, but Marcy seemed to be battling within herself as to whether or not she wanted to continue after the rescue.

Having been in a war and wounded, she felt uneasy about pressing her luck. After a lot of consideration, she agreed to complete the rescue part of the mission, but after that, she was finished.

Team two had reached a group decision, and were now awaiting the call from Mahoney. Team one had also reached their decision as well. In a matter of minutes, the call came. "Team three, teams one and two." Mahoney's voice came through.

"Team two copies," the radio operator replied.

"Team one copies," came a few seconds later as team one replied.

"Alright, team one what say you?" Mahoney asked.

After a few seconds the reply came. "Team one: a unanimous go, sir."

"Copy team one. Team two what say you?"

Bates took the radio and replied, "Team two is a go until the rescue is completed, and then we lose one sir. Just so you know, once we find and rescue our people, we will be sending that one plus three back to you. We will be short four after rescue. Do you copy?"

Damn it. Mahoney had not considered the fact that someone would need to accompany the hostages back to safety once they had been rescued. "Team two, standby please." Mahoney directed. "Team three, team one."

"Team one, copy."

"Teams one and two, I need you to maintain your current routes. Upon arrival at the final set of coordinates, I want both teams to stand down until further instructions," Mahoney instructed.

Once both teams copied, Bates handed the radio back to the operator and glanced around at the others. "Well, let's get a move on. We've wasted enough time here, and we've got some ground to make up." He turned and began walking once again, with everyone following.

At the same time, Mahoney took out a map of Iraq. He tried to locate an area where the two teams could join up once the rescue had been completed - if it could be completed. At this point, he still was not sure it could be done, or if the hostages were even at either location.

Kerchief had interrogated and attempted to initiate a response from Cayce. She gave no response to anything he said or did to her; it did not matter what he tried. At times, it did not seem like she even knew where she was. After receiving no reaction, he felt safe to conclude that she was broken, but now he would test her without restraints.

Cayce had receded far back into the deepest corners of her mind. She did not hear, feel, or see anything being done to or around her, nor did she care.

This was a potentially dangerous move on her part. Most of the patients she had treated in the past, who had resolved to do the same thing after a traumatic experience, were never able to fully come back to reality and assume a normal life again. Still, she felt that if she were to survive this and have any sanity left, that it was a risk she had no choice but to take.

She was taken back to her little room and left alone with her psychic guard. They placed the earphones back into her ears, but this time without music - this time it had a message. *"Death to the infidels and praise be to Allah."*

The message rang into her mind, and it repeated over and over, melting into a never ending nightmare. She sat in the corner with her knees against her chest and stared into oblivion.

A few doors down from her, three men entered. Shortly afterwards, muffled screams could be heard echoing off the warehouse walls once again.

Doc had been trying to sleep, but not knowing what was going to happen next kept him awake and aware. Without warning, the door to his room swung open, and someone entered.

He could not tell for sure, but it sounded like more than one person. He started to get that uneasy feeling, like this visit was not going to go well for him.

Just like the previous visits, they began to kick and beat him profusely while yelling in Arabic. He had already been beaten so badly that he could barely see, and his nose was so full of dried blood he could no longer breathe through it.

He was positive he had cracked ribs as well as a broken left arm. These beatings had become a daily ordeal for him and the other five captives. He could not figure out why they were keeping him alive; during the beatings he wished they would just end it.

One of the men hit Doc so hard that he fell to the floor, knocking out his earplugs and causing him to see stars. A round of kicks began to pound his body and head. He curled up into a fetal position to protect himself to no avail. His hands were still tied behind his back, so all he could do was try to curl up as much as he could as each kick found its mark.

After what seemed like an eternity, they stopped. One of the men got down on the floor and into Doc's face. "Do not worry my friend; your time will come soon and all your pain will cease. It would be over with one fell swoop of my sword." The man snickered as he rose from the floor and left the room with his comrades.

Doc lay on the floor in a dazed state, unable to move and unwilling to try. The pain was so intense and deep, he struggled to take in breath. Blood again began to trickle from his nose and mouth. This was the fourth beating since he had been taken captive; he was in bad shape and he knew it.

Jonas and team two were about a mile out from their coordinates. He was talking to Walt when all a sudden, Walt stopped as if being hit with a baseball bat. Marcy noticed and fell in beside Jonas as they began to fall to the back of the group.

"Start keeping an eye out and remember, whisper in my ear if someone notices or starts to approach us." Jonas whispered to Marcy.

Marcy went a little further up ahead of Jonas and Walt. Suddenly Walt doubled over in pain. *"D-Doc!"* he was finally able to say.

Jonas quickly began to concentrate on Doc's face, and before he knew it, he was seeing through Doc's eyes.

Doc was apparently blindfolded, for Jonas could not see anything except a few strands of light, but it did appear from his position he was on the floor. Jonas quickly attempted to jump out of Doc and above him to get a view of where he was. It took a little longer than the first trip had taken, but he did complete the jump.

Suddenly, the room came into view. Doc was lying on the floor with a bearded man yelling something to him as he remained motionless in a fetal position. Off to the side, two other men were watching with grins on their faces.

Jonas had a thought and concentrated on the man's face. He wanted to burn it into his mind. Within the blink of an eye, he tripped into the man, and was now viewing through his eyes. The man got back to his feet and the three of them walked out of the room, and into a long hallway.

The man glanced towards one end of the hall. Jonas noticed more doors, with men standing outside of them. Turning, the man headed the opposite direction.

Jonas noticed that the end of the hall opened up into what appeared to be a warehouse. A rush of excitement coursed over his body. He knew where they were being held: the warehouse in Al Salmon. Just as the man reached the area where it opened up, from out of nowhere Jonas heard a voice approaching.

Although he wanted – no, needed - to see Cayce, he reluctantly pulled back. In spite of his urge to stay connected, he now knew where they were. He also knew that if needed, he could trip back into that man again, whenever he wanted.

As for now, he had an established link, a link they would never suspect he had. He came out of the trip within seconds, and standing beside him was Bates. "I sure hope to hell you didn't just get someone killed," he stated with a pissed look on his face.

Jonas stood upright. "I wouldn't have taken the chance if I thought I would have. Besides, I now know where they are, and we're headed in the right direction."

"Are you positive? How can you be so sure?" Bates questioned.

"Because I saw them, or at least I saw Doc, and if he's there, the odds are the others are too," Jonas retorted.

Bates was bemused. This type of information gathering was way beyond his comprehension, and it was blowing his mind.

"Okay, if you're positive, let's get on the horn to Mahoney," he stated while staring at Jonas and trying to wrap his head around what just happened.

Moments after speaking to Jonas and Bates, Mahoney sat down in front of his laptop and pulled up Google maps once again. He searched the magnified picture of the compound, taking note of all the installations and towers. He needed an up-to-date picture to get a better plan of action, so he took out his cell and dialed Davy.

"Sorry to bother you sir, but have you been listening to the radio?" Mahoney asked the former president.

"Yes, I have, and I have already sent a message to a former chief of staff - who, by the way, is a very good friend of mine. I wanted to ask him if it were possible to send a drone over the area so we could get a clearer picture of what your people are up against. It should be over the area within an hour or so. I'll have the footage streamed to your laptop. I think it will prove to be most beneficial to you in your quest."

Mahoney was amazed at how much pull the former president still had, but then again he was well-liked during his tenure. "Yes, sir it most certainly will and once again, I thank you. Just a heads up: you may want to stay close to the radio; things are about to heat up."

"Colonel, I haven't left this radio since you got on your plane to fly over there. Stay in touch, and let me know if I can be of anymore service to you." Davy stated and hung up the phone.

Mahoney got back on the radio and called both teams to inform them of Davy's plan for the drone, and divert team one to team two's location.

Jonas was not at all happy about having to wait two hours before they got the word to move in, but he felt it better to at least wait for team one to catch up to them before attempting to move forward. He resolved that the hour or so difference was worth the extra help and Intel, so he decided to cool his heels until then.

IX: Deception

The warehouse was silent; everyone, except for the guards on watch and Cayce, were asleep. She sat in the same corner as always, waiting for her psychic guard to fall asleep as well.

The Black Sheik had underestimated her and left her hands unbound and her eyes uncovered. Thinking they had broken her, he did not think it was a necessity any longer; he was wrong on both counts.

The psychic guard sat in the only chair in the tiny room. He leaned back against the wall with his eyes closed, but still awake. Cayce sat motionless in her corner waiting for a sign that he had fallen asleep.

She waited, and finally heard the soft sound of snoring in between the loud chanting coming from the earphones.

Slowly she removed the earplugs from her ears. She had to make certain that the guard was incapacitated, so he would not get wind of any signal coming into her and warn anyone. The tiny room was dark, but she was sure there was not anything there she could use as a weapon, besides the chair.

"So the chair it will be," she said to herself as she rose to her feet. The front legs of the chair were off the floor, due to him leaning back, and she slowly bent over to grab them.

She was in a much weakened state and hoped she had enough power left to pull the chair from under him. Nonetheless, she had to do it; there was no other choice.

In one fell swoop, she pulled with all her might. The guard was caught completely by surprise. His eyes flew wide open as he slid down the wall to the floor.

Cayce brought the chair over her head and down on the guard. The chair broke into several pieces as it hit him squarely in the skull knocking him out cold. He lay slumped over, motionless.

Cayce drew in a deep breath and stood there looking at him while listening for possible approaching footsteps, but the warehouse remained silent.

Less than a mile away, Jonas and his group had stopped to make camp while waiting for team one to show. Jonas was getting antsy; he wanted to move in and get to Cayce. He knew she was in there; he could feel her and almost smell her perfume in the cool night air. It was killing him.

The second set of coordinates was in an area full of dunes, about three quarters of a mile southwest of the town of Al Salmon. Jonas gazed towards the small town. He could see slight glimmers of light off in the distance and his thoughts went to Cayce.

Without warning, a set of hands grabbed him from behind by the shoulders and yanked him down behind the dune. A small pickup truck rounded the dune ahead of them with a searchlight scanning back and forth. A mounted a machinegun turret and three men were in the back of the truck.

After he was able to catch his breath, Jonas realized it was Bates who grabbed him and stopped. Bates looked at him and with his index finger to his lips. He motioned for Jonas to come with him, and they peered over the dune.

They watched as the truck circled and disappeared in the distance. "Patrol units," Bates whispered, motioning for Jonas to follow him back down to the camp.

The group loosely gathered around in a small circle when Bates and Jonas arrived. Bates motioned for everyone to close in around him. "We have patrol units in the area," he said in a hushed tone. "No lights of any kind. Keep the talking down to a whisper and everyone keep a close eye out." He nodded to his men who ran off to take positions around the camp. "Now we wait."

Cayce paced around the room like a caged animal. She had had a plan, but she had not planned it all the way through and now she was not sure what to do. She did not have a psychic ability to contact anyone and screaming was out of the question.

She had to calm down and get her thoughts together, and she had to do it fast. She knew that when they found out what she had done, they would surely kill her.

She began to think back on all the accounts she had been witnessed during Stargate, and tried to recall what to do to open herself up to being sensed. Emotion was one main ingredient, but what else? She was so scared she could not think straight enough for it to come to her.

She paced and it finally hit her: calmness and an open mind. She sat down and began to meditate.

Jeff, Franks, and the rest of team one were en route to meet team two. However, they too had encountered patrol units casing the area. It was slow going and they would be pushing it to make it to team two's location before sunrise.

Jeff had received the same impression from Doc that Walt had, and he was startled by what he sensed. Doc would not be able to withstand much more; he was small and frail in stature to begin with. He was all mind, not muscle. It only enraged Jeff more to see what was taking place with his friends.

Franks and Jeff were sitting in the front seat of the truck. Jeff was going over the foldout map of the area, trying to figure out the best vantage points for entry into the compound.

"So team two is currently located here." Jeff pointed out an area on the map just southwest of Al Salmon. "We are going to be located here." He pointed to the northeast area of the town.

"Team one will create a diversion with team two so that we, the psychics, can enter from this location. With any luck, it will be enough of a diversion that we can basically enter without much or any resistance. Am I correct?"

Franks surreptitiously grinned at Jeff and studied the map for a few seconds before replying. "That's pretty much it, and to me it sounds like a solid plan. Why? Do you have doubts?"

Jeff deliberated for a couple of seconds. "No, I just wanted to make sure of what we were doing. I have no planning experience in battle situations, and I leave it up to people who know how to do it."

Franks glanced back at Jeff. "No harm, no foul; everyone's input is valuable. So don't stop giving input. You just might hit on something of importance that may help us out or that we didn't consider." Jeff nodded in acknowledgement and continued studying the map.

Ten minutes later, Jeff and Walt simultaneously began received a vision. At first it was unclear as to whom it was coming from. They both struggled to determine the origin, but one thing was for sure: someone had opened the door to their mind.

Jonas was sitting by himself contemplating his own course of action when Marcy came darting up to him. He got to his feet as she approached and without giving her a chance to speak asked, "Who is it?"

Marcy glanced around to make sure no one was within listening range and replied. "He's not sure yet, but something was coming across to him. You may want to come with me right now." She turned and headed back to Walt, and Jonas followed.

By the time they reached Walt, he and Jeff realized it was Cayce. Walt was ecstatic and blurted it out all at once when Jonas approached.

Instantly, Jonas began to trip into Cayce. The connection was so strong he almost did not realize that he had tripped into her. It was the quickest he had ever tripped into anyone.

Cayce remained in the center of the room with her eyes closed, not knowing that Jonas had tripped into her. He quickly realized this and sent a thought into her mind. She opened her eyes, not knowing why.

Jonas could see, but it was dark and indistinguishable, not to mention small. He sent another thought into her mind to stand and walk about the room. Again she did, not knowing why.

She was confused, and kept telling herself she wanted to be sitting on the floor, sitting with an open mind so someone could reach her. Suddenly she began to wonder if someone was in her mind.

She quickly began to write something on the floor in the sand. *In an old warehouse, not sure where, many men with black sheik, come quickly, we are all now in great danger.*

As Jonas read what she wrote, he struggled against the urge to cut the connection and run towards the small town. Fear welled up inside of him, as he worried for her life.

He needed to get to her, but he also needed more information, such as where they were being kept in the warehouse and how many are standing guard over them. He sent the thought into her mind again, and she wrote *N. E. corner* and *maybe twenty or thirty.*

His love for her overwhelmed him; he wanted to let her know that he was on his way. He could not think straight anymore; his emotions were overriding his thought process. He fought to get it under control, but it was too much for him.

Wave after wave of sadness and hopelessness, followed by a huge surge of love swept over him. Struggling to keep control, he lost the connection, and with it, he lost Cayce.

He came out of the trip after a few seconds and found everyone congregated around him. Tears were streaming down his face as he choked out, "She's there and we have no time to waste. We've got to hurry."

Exhausted, he collapsed where he stood. He was confused as to why it had taken so much out of him to trip this time, but he felt weary and worn out. Walt and Marcy ran to his side and sat him upright as he wavered back and forth.

Bates rushed over and knelt beside him, "Can you tell me what you saw?"

Jonas glanced up and took a deep breath. "It's the warehouse, twenty to thirty men guarding." He paused as he was regaining his strength. "That bastard Kerchief is also there."

Bates put a comforting hand on Jonas' shoulder. "That's all I needed to know. I'll get on the horn to Mahoney and work out a plan. Great job, Jonas."

A few minutes later Jonas, Walt, and Marcy began to concoct their plan of action while Bates spoke to Mahoney.

The goal was to work in conjunction with the main assault plan if possible, but if not - if Bates decided to wait on team one to show before making a move - then so be it. Jonas was forging ahead with it regardless; he would wait no longer.

Meanwhile, the small dime-sized white patch that had developed on the sides of each temple had grown to double its original size.

Cayce was feeling a spark of hope that maybe she - or at least the others - would make it out alive after all. She contemplated what to do next. The guard would be awakening soon and the alarm would go off when they realized what she had done.

The events that would follow concerned her to no end. Would they execute her? Would they make an example of her? Would they kill the others and make her watch?

She feared the worst, but it no longer mattered what happened to her. It was the rest of the group that mattered. If her actions got help here to free them, she felt she had accomplished her goal.

As long as they were safe, she did not care what they did to her. She would face whatever consequences came her way. Her thoughts went to Jonas and how she loved him, wondering if he really knew just how much.

The guard began to stir. She quickly erased the message in the sand and went back to her corner. She glanced back at the slumped over guard, who was slowly stirring, sat down, and began to once again recede to the back of her mind. Back where they could not touch her.

_____

Team one was still an hour out, but they were making better time. The patrol units they had encountered had thinned out. With that, and the fact that Jeff was able to sense other people around the area, it was possible to make up lost time by detouring around where he sensed there were people. Franks, like Bates, was totally in the dark about the form of communication, or sensing, that had been taking place.

He had seen some strange shit before, like voodoo and black magic, but that all paled in comparison to the shit he was witnessing now. He was completely awestruck by the accuracy and detail from each vision, right down to the feelings of whoever was being sensed.

Except for the display in the shanty, he had yet to see Jonas in action, and he could only imagine the prospect of seeing a different location through someone else's eyes. The whole concept was flat out mind-boggling to him.

Jeff rode with his eyes closed and concentrated on anything within the area they were headed to. With any luck, the coast would stay clear until they arrived at team two's location.

Franks listened to the conversation between Bates and Mahoney. When Bates announced that Jonas had been in contact with Cayce, it broke Jeff's concentration, and he too began to listen.

Back at the little shanty, Mahoney listened to what Bates had to say. In the middle of the conversation, he stopped Bates. "Hold that thought for a second will you please. I want to make sure team one is listening." After waiting a second or two he called out to team one.

"Team three, team one over," he said into the radio.

After a few seconds, team one responded. "Team one, team three do you copy?"

"Team one, have you been listening?" Mahoney asked.

"Team one, team three. Yes, we have. Sounds like good news so far."

Mahoney nodded to himself. "Team one, keep listening. I will need input after the briefing is completed."

"Roger, wilco sir."

"Alright you may continue," Mahoney responded to Bates.

Bates did, and after several minutes of explaining what had transpired, he finished by saying, "Sir, if I hadn't seen it with my own eyes, I wouldn't have believed it."

Mahoney chuckled to himself. "Yes, I know that feeling well. Okay, let's get down to the business of working out an attack plan. Team one do you have any input?"

Over the course of the next fifteen minutes the three of them - Mahoney, Bates and Franks - discussed the best way to approach the target and get their people out, with minimal loss.

When it was all said and done, the three agreed that the preliminary plan would stay in place for the time being. Upon arrival at team two's location, team one, minus the psychics in that group, would move to the northeast area from the compound. Team two would stay put at the southwest corner and all the psychics from team one and two would move to the northwest.

Once everyone was in place, both Bates and Franks would lay down diversion fire to draw out the terrorist to the northeast and southwest corners of the compound.

This diversion was intended to give the psychics the opportunity to get into the compound from the northwest without much resistance. This plan would only work if everything was as Mahoney hoped it would be when the drone made its pass. If not, it was back to the drawing board.

By the time team one finally rendezvoused with team two, the drone should have made its pass and they would know for sure. Until then, it was the plan they intended to use.

The alarm sounded in the warehouse, bringing it to life. Men scampered in every direction trying to figure out what had happened. Kerchief and his enforcers entered Cayce's room where the psychic guard was standing holding his head.

Kerchief turned and approached the guard. "Are you alright my friend?" he asked seeming concerned.

The guard, believing Kerchief to be concerned, replied, "Yes Sheik, I am fine," as he slightly bowed to Kerchief.

"Good, good," Kerchief stated. "How did this happen? How is it that a psychic has let a weakling female get the drop on him? Answer me!" he bellowed in frustration.

The guard was stunned by the sudden change, and was at a loss for words, managing only to stutter out a few unrecognizable words when trying to respond.

"I'll tell you how," Kerchief continued. "You, my friend, were not watching her. You were sleeping. *Tell me it's not so!*" He was becoming angrier with every passing second the guard remained in his sight.

The guard lowered his head in disgrace as Kerchief removed his blade from its sheath, and in one swift move, sliced the guard's throat. Blood gushed everywhere as the man grabbed his throat trying to stop the bleeding. In a matter of seconds, he fell to the floor motionless.

Kerchief wiped his blade off on the man's robe and sheathed his blade. He turned to his enforcers. "Bring her and the rest of the prisoners to the center of the warehouse floor," he instructed his men, turning and walking out the door towards the main floor of the warehouse.

The main enforcer with the dark beard and blue eyes snatched Cayce up so violently it nearly dislocated her arms. She was thankfully in her safe place and hardly noticed as he pushed her out in front of him and forced her to move.

One by one, each member of the kidnapped group was brought to the center of the warehouse floor. Once again, Cayce did not show any emotion or signs of recognition as each of them tried to call for her.

Once everyone was brought to the center, Kerchief sat in the only chair. All of the terrorists, except for the tower guards, surrounded the small group.

Kerchief began to address his men. "I have tried to inform each of you as to the deception of these infidels - their lack of values, their lack of belief in Mohammad and Allah. Now I will show you of their deception, and I will show you how I deal with such deception."

Two of the three enforcers dragged in the body of the psychic guard that had been watching over Cayce and dropped him in the middle with the prisoners.

"This is what their deception can cause," Kerchief continued. "This is what happens when you believe what they say or how they act. This man is now dead because of this woman, this infidel. This is what their disbelief brings to us; this is the curse they bring and why they must die."

Everyone broke out into a chant: *"Death to the infidels… Death to the infidels… Death to the infidels…"*

Kerchief stood up and lowered his hands to quieten everyone down. "I know they must die and they will. But, I have a plan in place and for that reason death must wait for them. But the time will come that they will pay for their indiscretions and we, the Brotherhood, will be their saviors, we will take them along the trail of death. This I promise you."

The warehouse exploded into a frantic applause and chants of praise to the Sheik. Once again Kerchief raised his hands, and everyone got quiet. "After Fajr we will punish the female while her comrade's watch. Then they will know not to deceive us as she has done. Praise be to Mohammad and Allah." Thunderous joy erupted once again, and the chants resumed.

X: The Incursion

Aljeb had been standing off to the side while Jonas, Walt, and Marcy made plans and discussed what the next move was. When the group had finished, Aljeb approached them before they could break up and rejoin the main group.

"If you will pardon me," he stated nervously, "I have overheard what you have been speaking of and it is a good plan, but… I do see weaknesses."

"And what might they be?" Jonas responded incredulously.

Aljeb noticed the sarcasm in his tone, but ignored it. "How will you will understand what is being asked of you once you enter the compound? Have you given thought to the time on which you choose to enter?"

The smug look disappeared from Jonas' face. After giving it considerable thought, he answered, "I guess you have a point. So what would you have us to do?"

Aljeb smiled. "Simple: you will need to take me with you. I will translate for you and if they say something that they know you will comprehend, I will know it and inform you. You can never be too careful of these people. I would also make the incursion during Fajr. They will not be expecting you during prayer time, so you can catch them off guard."

Jonas nodded his head. "Okay, I see your point on taking you in with us and I'm assuming that Fajr is the Morning Prayer, am I correct?" Aljeb nodded. "So what time do they have Fajr?"

Aljeb glanced down at his watch. "It will be just before sunrise, which I believe is in about an hour and ten minutes."

Jonas thought on this. "Okay, first we go see what the main group has planned, and if it's not running with our plan, we leave in forty minutes to head for the northwest corner of the compound. If it's something we can work with, then we join them on the assault. Any questions?" No one raised their voice, so they left to rejoin the main group.

Bates finished with Mahoney and Franks, and in the midst of gathering everyone to share the gist of the plan, Jonas, Aljeb, and the other psychics rejoined the group.

"Everyone come in close," Bates began. "We don't want to be heard or spotted by the terrorists. I

147

have just finished consulting with Mahoney and Franks on a preliminary plan of assault, and now I will pass it on to you."

The group moved in closer as he spoke. "Bear in mind, it's just a preliminary plan and it may change depending on what the drone shows us on its pass. At any rate, it's what we have. When team one arrives at our location, they will take the northeast corner of the compound. We - team two - will remain here at the southwest corner while the psychics will move to the northwest corner.

"Once everyone is in place, teams one and two will lay out diversion fire to give the psychics a clear entry into the compound. At that point, we will use the LAWS (Lightweight Armor Weapons) to take out any armed vehicles within the compound. Once they are eliminated, we move. It will be the psychics' job to locate and rescue the hostages. Our job is simply to back them up with supporting fire."

Jonas spoke up asking, "Have you determined the time this will take place?"

Bates glance his way, "As of now it will be whenever team one arrives."

Jonas moved in closer. "I ask because Aljeb brought up a good point: if we hit them during Fajr, we will catch them off guard and it will increase our chances of success. However, at this time, we only have an hour until Fajr starts. How soon before team one arrives?"

Bates glanced at his watch. "I'm not sure, but I'll get on the horn and find out."

"When do we, the psychics, start to move into position?" Jonas inquired.

Bates had calculated this and decided to get them moving immediately. He would send over the other psychics from team one as soon as they arrived. He instructed Jonas to get his people and get moving.

Bates turned towards the group. "For now, I want everyone else to check over their weapons and get some rest. Be prepared when we're ready to move." The group dispersed, and Bates approached Jonas. "You ok?"

Jonas looked him in the eyes and replied, "I'll be better when we get in there and get our people." Bates nodded in agreement.

Team one was about thirty-five minutes out from team two's location. They had been fortunate not to run into any other patrol units in the area, allowing them to make up a little time. Jeff sensed the area in front and around them for anything that may be another patrol, but he was also sensing something else. He could not nail it down, but it was something. All he knew was that something was not right.

Franks was scanning out the window when Bates called for team one on the radio requesting an ETA. He was not exactly sure what time they would arrive, but he believed it would be around thirty to thirty-five minutes.

Will, Marcy and Aljeb were checking their weapons when Jonas approached. "We pull out in five," Jonas announced. The three acknowledged with a head nod and continued checking their weapons.

They set off north, taking a wide sweeping berth to the west and staying behind the dunes, and planned to sweep back east into position at the northwest corner. Jonas asked Marcy to send a message to Gill, the telepath in team one, and tell them that they were headed to their assault position, and instruct them to join once they arrived.

The four of them moved swiftly, remaining hidden from anyone in the compound. They only had twenty minutes to arrive at the northwest corner and get organized.

That would leave them ten minutes before Fajr started and the attack began. Jonas was anxious, and the closer he got to their position, the more anxious he became.

Bates positioned his team on the back side of the nearest dune, placing the LAW where it had a full view of the compound. He set up the M-60 machinegun next to it, giving it a full view of the compound. He and the other six members would move around behind the dune to wherever they were needed.

Inside the compound, two of the off duty psychics dashed towards Kerchief's office. They banged on the door and impatiently waited for a reply.

"Enter!" the reply came in Arabic. They quickly opened the door and rushed to the front of the desk. Kerchief remained seated wondering what they wanted, and when neither spoke up, he grew frustrated. "Well? What is it?"

The older of the two stepped forward and stated in Arabic, "We have sensed something. Something is not right."

Kerchief stood and gave him a quizzical look. "What do you mean something is not right?"

The older man shied back in fear of Kerchief and retorted, "We are not exactly sure, but we are sensing danger nearby."

Instantly, Kerchief yelled for his enforcers. "Get everyone outside and stand watch. Something is about to happen. Get a vehicle ready for me to leave. I will go to Al-Kasrah and await news from you."

Within seconds, the compound was swirling with movement as the terrorists took up positions. The tall enforcer with the reddish beard pulled the black SUV, which was parked inside the warehouse, up to the inside of the roll-up door.

The shorter enforcer with the blue eyes stayed with Kerchief as he packed important papers and prepared to leave.

The enforcer asked Kerchief what to do with the prisoners. Kerchief stopped packing. "The woman comes with me, as for the rest... *Kill them all!*" The enforcer nodded his acceptance of the order and left the room.

Team one was five minutes out. They had stopped momentarily to drop off the psychic group who set out on foot to join Jonas and his group. As Franks and the remaining members of team one arrived at team two's location, Bates notified Mahoney that they were onsite and would be in position within ten minutes.

Jonas and his team of psychics arrived at their destination. Franks and team one moved into position while Bates, along with the rest of team, two were in position and ready. Bates suddenly noticed the activity within the compound.

"Damn, they know something's up," he stated under his breath.

He hoped that Jonas and his team had noticed; if not, it could prove to be hazardous. He feared that if the terrorists suspected something, the plan to attack during Fajr would be out the window. They would have to play it by ear.

Jonas noticed the activity, and rather than assume as to what was happening, he opted to use his connection to the enforcer that he had tripped into earlier. He wanted to see what was happening inside the warehouse. He closed his eyes and began to concentrate, and within seconds, he was viewing through the man's eyes.

He found himself standing in a small office, his gaze following Kerchief around as he packed papers and other material into a satchel. Kerchief was speaking to him in Arabic. Jonas could not understand the conversation, but it seemed that he was adamant about what he was saying.

Kerchief turned and walked out of the room towards the SUV. The view followed him and then changed from Kerchief to the center of the warehouse floor.

There, he saw Cayce, Doc, and the remaining five of their team, bound and on their knees. The view went back to Kerchief once again; he watched as Kerchief put the satchel into the SUV while speaking to the driver.

"He's planning to run," thought Jonas as he continued watching. Kerchief turned to the man and began to speak while pointing to the hostages. Jonas had a feeling they were discussing the fate of the hostages.

A strong sense of urgency instantly filled his thoughts, but he did not know what to do. They could not force their way into the warehouse by themselves. They had to get into position and be ready. Any waste of time could mean the death of any one of the hostages.

He began to pull back, leaving a thought inside the man's mind. He hoped it would work to their advantage when the time came to attack. He was not sure it would last that long, but he needed to try something to give them an advantage.

He rejoined his team members, and, after a lengthy discussion, the realization hit that they had no way of contacting Bates - or anyone else for that matter, an oversight that could cost them in a big way. Marcy volunteered to make the trip back and inform

Bates of what Jonas had seen. He could only hope she made it back before Bates and Franks let loose with the diversion.

In the meantime, he would take Walt and Aljeb, heading towards the north tower. Jeff and Robert, who had just arrived, would head for the east tower. There they would wait for the diversion to start. Once the guard's attention was focused towards the action, they would approach and take them out.

As to what to do about Kerchief making a run for it, Jonas decided to let him go. The hostages were the first priority, he had to get to them and free them first; he had to get to Cayce.

Bates was on the radio with Mahoney when Marcy came running up to him. She had made it back to Bates in record time, due, in part, to her being an advent runner in her spare time.

Bates saw her as she approached and spoke into the radio. "Hold one, sir! I think we may have a problem." He turned his attention to Marcy who bent over to catch her breath.

Marcy glanced up at Bates. "Jonas tripped. They know something's going on and Kerchief is prepping to make a run for it. We had no radio to contact you so…"

"Damn it! That was my mistake. I just took for granted that your entire group was telepathic," Bates said in frustration. He rejoined Mahoney and informed him of the changes.

"We can't worry about Kerchief right now. We must concentrate on getting our people out of there first. Kerchief will just have to wait," Mahoney instructed.

The frustration of not getting Kerchief when he was right within their grasp was, to say the least, bad fucking luck.

"Sir, Fajr is due to begin in less than three minutes," Bates added. "If they do not begin their prayer at that time, we begin the diversion. Either way the fireworks start in three."

The aerial photos from the drone came across Mahoney's laptop, and from the looks of it, everything was still the same inside the compound, meaning everything was a go.

Mahoney acknowledged and replied, "Good luck Captain."

Bates chuckled into the radio. "Sir, luck has nothing to do with it. We just need to be on key for this song to play our way."

"Roger that!" Mahoney agreed.

Somewhere in the middle of the small town, a bell rang, and over the loudspeaker a voice recited Fajr. Bates watched the compound, searching for signs of joining in Fajr. Each member stood their ground in wait, expecting something to happen.

Bates, not being one to let anyone down, gave the signal to oblige with a response. The early morning sky lit up with gunfire and missiles as both teams let go of everything in their arsenal.

The distinct sounds of the AK-47 filled the air as the M-60 machineguns sang backup, and in between, the LAW missiles made themselves known with an awful tearing sound as they ripped through dense morning air.

As expected, all attention turned towards the gunfire, and that gave Jonas, Jeff and their group the time they needed to reach the bottom of each perspective tower.

As each of the guards focused on the location of the gunfire, Jonas pulled his .45 out and took aim. The report of the .45 was deafening as it sent a bullet through the back of the guards head. He slumped and fell over the railing to the ground. Jeff took out the guard in his tower, and both teams headed for the gate.

Bates' and Frank's teams took out the guards in the other towers along with three of the four vehicles in the compound. Everyone, except for two men who were sprinting toward the gate, had migrated towards the eastern side to confront the onslaught facing them.

Jonas reached the gate just as the men were opening it. Without warning, a black SUV blew past him so close, it knocked him on his ass. One of the men noticed Jonas fall and drew a bead on him.

A barrage of gunfire erupted from behind him, and the two men fell to the ground. Jonas jumped back to his feet and turned to find Jeff and Robert, who had arrived just as Jonas had fallen.

Jonas nodded his head to them, turned, and sprinted towards the warehouse door while the others followed. When they reached the side of the building, they stopped. Jonas turned to face the others and motioned with two fingers towards his eyes, and set out across the compound. They all nodded and began to keep watch as Jonas tripped into the enforcer again.

Within an instant, he was once again viewing through the enforcer's eyes. The enforcer and two other men were beating the hostages with long clubs. This infuriated Jonas to the point that he, without thinking, sent a painful thought into the enforcer.

The pain hit his brain with a force that knocked him five feet backwards and onto the dirt floor. At that instant, he jumped out of the enforcer and into an overhead view of the warehouse floor. He could see the enforcer lying on the floor convulsing while the other two men gawked in confusion.

He turned his sights to the hostages. They were badly beaten and bloody. A few were rolling around on the floor, and one or two were not moving at all. Suddenly, terror struck him as he realized Cayce was not there.

He scanned again to make sure he did not miss her, but to no avail. He began to panic; his pulse quickened, and he began to lose his train of thought. He felt himself slipping out of the trip. Quickly, he sent a thought into the enforcer's mind and he came out of the trip.

Everyone stared at him, fear covering their faces. "What happened?" cried Jeff as his right eye began to twitch.

Jonas, as if waking from a nightmare, snapped his head around to Jeff and sprinted toward the warehouse roll-up door. Bemused, Jeff and the others followed. He suddenly stopped just short of the opening.

Outside the compound, Bates, Franks, and their crew were making their way into the confines of the compound. They had disposed of most of the terrorists, and those they had not disposed of fled into the town and surrounding buildings.

It would only be a matter of seconds before they would have the compound secure, at which point they could locate and support Jonas and his crew if needed.

XI. Sand Snakes and Lizards

Kerchief was getting away. His driver had been hauling flat out since pulling out of the warehouse and would not let up until they reached Al-Kasrah.

Since his hasty departure from the United States a year prior, he maintained contact with the sleepers he left there. They were his ace in the hole, and it was time to use them.

He felt he had enough sleepers to do the job, but due to losses over time, the method of delivery would need to change as well as the targets. Walking past security with a concealed bomb would not do this time.

This time they would need to hit fast and repeatedly until the targets were taken out. As for the time being, he would contact them and have them prepared to strike upon a moment's notice. When the time came, he would give them the targets.

"The United States was foolish to think I would play the game without stacking the deck," he stated to himself as he typed out a group text and hit send.

Mahoney listened to the chatter between Bates and Franks as the battle raged. It worried him that Jonas and his team had no means of communication with them. Something could go horribly wrong, and he would be in the dark about it.

He wrung his hands in anticipation, waiting to hear someone to say the compound was secure, and the hostages had been liberated.

With his ears glued to the radio, he was startled when his cell began to ring. Without looking, he answered. "Team three!" he blurted out, irritation in his voice. He cooled his heels when Davy's voice came across.

"Sorry to bother you at this particular time Colonel, but I thought you might like to know that help is on the way. The United States has an air strike in route to Al-Kasrah as we speak. Crawford's beheading gave them an excuse to do something they've wanted to do for a long time. They should be in theater within the next hour and fifteen.

"I also thought I should share that I received a call from Bill Winters. He has informed me that Jim Stafford and his team from the NSA intercepted a text message. It was very short and vague, but he feels that it may have sent by Kerchief, and possibly carrying a signal word to tell the sleepers to be ready. Kerchief has now switched to plan 'B' and fled the scene in that black SUV.

"Winters and his team are working to track down the receiving numbers for that text, and are setting up task forces to capture them once there're located. You just concentrate on your end of things and let people in the States worry about what's happening over here. I do hope you know that, regardless of the outcome, I thank you and your team for your great effort."

"Thank you, sir," Mahoney replied. "By the time the air strikes arrive, the incursion will be finished and the hostages rescued. I do find the group mail to be interesting though. It's becoming clear to me that this was his plan to begin with, and this was all an oversized diversion to draw our attention away from the sleepers.

"Unfortunately, that also means it's now imperative that we catch and stop him. As for your last statement, sir, it has been and always will be our pleasure to serve you," and with that, the call ended.

Inside the warehouse, the main enforcer had recovered from Jonas' attack, and was back on his feet. Dazed and unsure of what had happened to him, he gathered his thoughts before continuing the beatings.

Aljeb devised a plan to enter the warehouse and draw the guard's attention while the rest of the team positioned themselves. His thought was to run in and act as though he was with the terrorist group while shouting that the sheik had been captured just outside of town. The hope was that this would confuse the terrorists long enough to stop the beatings so the group could surround them.

As he began to enter, a door at the far end of the building swung open, and out ran a group of ten to fifteen men. Jonas swung around and was just about to tweak the trigger when he noticed they had no weapons and posed no threat. Fear covered their faces as they raced through the gate and into the town.

The group turned back to Aljeb. He nodded his head, turned, and rushed into the warehouse screaming in Arabic. Inside, everyone froze. The terrorists were caught off guard at first, but as Aljeb yelled, they quickly assumed he was one of theirs and began to ask questions. He had their attention.

Jonas and the rest of the group rushed through the doorway. Robert took out the other enforcer with a single shot; Walt took out the other man as he stood with a confused look on his face. Jonas glared at the lone enforcer, and as their eyes met, the thought that Jonas had previously implanted within his brain, began influencing him.

The enforcer dropped his weapon and dropped to his knees, staring at Jonas. Raising his hands above his head, he bowed, keeping his arms out stretched. His palms touched the dirt floor with each bow, while speaking in Arabic.

Confused, Aljeb glanced at the enforcer and back at Jonas, and after a few seconds, he approached Jonas and inquired, "Why does he call you Allah? Has he gone mad?"

Jonas grinned. "Never mind why. We need information... *I* need information. I need you to translate what he says."

"You are amazing. I am stunned with your abilities," Aljeb stated, and he began to translate.

Bates, Franks, and the rest of the team entered the building while Jeff, Walt, and Robert checked on the hostages. Doc was badly beaten along with three of the others, but unfortunately, two had succumbed to their injuries.

Bates and Franks approached Jonas and Aljeb as they questioned the enforcer. At first, the enforcer seemed to be fighting the notion of answering, but quickly changed his mind when Jonas stepped towards him and raised his voice.

"Where did Kerchief take the woman?" Jonas questioned, as his gaze remained locked onto the enforcer's stare.

Aljeb listened to the response, and turning to Jonas, he replied, "Al-Kasrah; he's taken her to Al-Kasrah."

"What are his plans upon arriving?" Jonas asked.

"Kerchief is waiting for word as to what happens here, and then he would take the woman north to the city of Al Bukamal in Syria. There, she would be sold as a sex slave to the men fighting to take the city."

Jonas remained stone-faced, even though he wanted to rip off this asshole's face. Finally, after forcing his emotions down, he asked what he wanted to know most: "Who raped the woman?"

Aljeb froze; he remembered how Jonas reacted when he had gotten the news of the rape and he feared a reprisal. He stared at Jonas unsure whether he should continue.

"Well?" Jonas snapped at him.

Aljeb waited for the answer. "He said that it was the sheik, himself, and two other enforcers, one of which lies dead over there on the floor and the other with the sheik."

The fire began to show in Jonas' eyes. The rage and hatred for this man and what he stood for reached a dangerous level as he fought to contain it.

He glanced at the enforcer and made one last statement. "What you have done has disappointed Allah, and for that you will rot in the fires of hell."

The statement stunned Aljeb. The man cried out in desperation as he crawled towards Jonas on his knees.

"He says he was only doing what he thought was your wish and begs for your forgiveness," Aljeb translated.

Jonas thought for a second. "If you truly want my forgiveness, call the sheik and tell him to return with the woman. Fail and I will send you to hell myself."

The enforcer rapidly bowed to Jonas as he took out his cell and dialed a number. After a moment, Kerchief's phone began to ring. He glanced at the caller ID and wondered why his enforcer would be calling him.

"I hope you are calling to say the compound is still under your control," Kerchief stated as he put the phone to his ear. Almost at once, the enforcer began pleading with Kerchief to return with the woman. For a solid two minutes, Kerchief was unable to get a single word into the conversation.

Finally, out of frustration he yelled into the phone. "Shut up you idiot!" Silence returned from the other end.

Trying to cut him off, Kerchief received very little from the enforcer. It seemed to him that Allah was there. "Tell me of this foolishness that you are speaking. What do you mean Allah is there?"

169

Once again, the enforcer began to explain what was happening, but remained much calmer and got his message across to Kerchief. He knew in his own mind that either the enforcer had lost his wits or someone was masquerading as Allah. He was willing to bet on the latter.

"I wish to speak to Allah," Kerchief said. The enforcer stammered, unsure whether he should hand the phone over. He glanced up at Jonas and stated, "He wishes to speak to you, Lord."

Jonas took the phone. "Hello, Kerchief."

Kerchief knew it was not Allah; this man was speaking English. "To whom do I have the pleasure of speaking?" Kerchief asked in a cynical tone.

"What? Do you not recognize Allah when you hear him? I thought you spoke to him daily is that not true?" Jonas replied in an even more cynical tone.

Kerchief paused and laughed at this comment. "Well, you see that is true, but I do not think I am speaking to Allah. I think you are a fool masquerading as my Lord, and you have somehow fooled my men. So tell me, who are you?"

Jonas paused, and began to tell a story: "Once upon a time I was just a man trying to make a living. Now, due to unstable fanatics like you, I have become your worst nightmare. I am the remote viewer you asked for, and I am going to be your executioner."

Kerchief found himself at a loss for words as silence filled the airwaves. After a few seconds, he found his tongue again. "So you did come! I am surprised. So, tell me Mr. Viewer…why? Do these people mean so much to you that you are willing to risk your own life to rescue them? Or is it just one life that concerns you?"

Jonas was stunned into silence, wondering how Kerchief had put the pieces together.

"So Mr. Viewer man, what may I call you? Kerchief asked indignantly.

Feeling crossed by the question, Jonas replied, "Call me Jonas."

"Very well Jonas, we must talk. What is it you want other than the female?" Kerchief asked.

"Let's stop beating around the bush and get to the point!" Jonas blasted into the phone. "You know the female is what I came for, and I know you want me.

So let's cut the bullshit and make a swap: me for the woman."

Kerchief remained quiet for several seconds before replying. "But what of my men? They will miss out on such a fine woman; it will break their hearts not to have her. Do you think I should refuse them that pleasure?" Kerchief was enjoying this part of the conversation while Jonas was getting pissed.

Jonas became annoyed with the situation and fired back at Kerchief. "You began this when you kidnapped my friends. You had conditions you wanted met in order to set them free. I was one of those conditions. Now either you want me or you don't. Either way I will find you, and when I do, it might go easier on you if you make the exchange."

Kerchief found this statement to be humorous and laughed, bringing Jonas to the edge of his self-control. "If you think I can't get to you, think again. I'll prove to you I am who I say I am," Jonas barked into the phone. He closed his eyes and pictured Kerchief's face. Within an instant, he was viewing through Kerchief's eyes.

He began to speak once again. "You are sitting in the back of seat of the SUV. I can see your driver and the area outside your window. Right now, you are looking around to see if anyone is following you. Now I will put a thought into your head. You may try to fight it, but it will be too strong an urge, and you will comply. This will be proof that I am who I say I am, and I can get to you whenever I want."

Jonas planted the thought into Kerchief's mind to stop the vehicle, which he did. He checked on Cayce before getting out and looking to the sky. He scanned the area around himself.

After a few minutes Kerchief resumed talking, "I fail to see what you're trying to pull. I have not done anything out of the ordinary."

"Maybe not," Jonas stated, "but I will tell you what you did, and I will also tell you why you did it."

Kerchief found this to be amusing. He sat back into the SUV and told his driver to continue onward. "Very well," he replied. "Tell me what you think I have done and why."

Jonas detailed his every move. Uncertainty filled Kerchief's mind as he slapped the back of the driver's seat and yelled for the driver to stop the vehicle. When Jonas finished, only silence remained.

Kerchief sat quietly for several seconds in thought. *Could it be that this man was the viewer? How else could he have known what he had done in so much detail?* Posing a swap could work to his advantage, but only if Jonas was willing to do his bidding afterwards.

It could also be a trap; if he planted a thought into his mind, and he followed that thought without knowing he did, then this man had the potential to control his mind and that could prove to be dangerous to him. He had to be sure.

"Very well, I will consider a swap. Meet me in Al-Kasrah in one hour. Come alone and don't be late. If I so much as see a dog near you, the woman will die. I will personally see to it myself." The line went dead as Kerchief pushed end on his cell.

Jonas stood in silence for several seconds before Bate approached him. "What that was all about, or may I even ask?" he questioned as Franks arrived beside him.

Jonas knew the best thing would be to lie to them, and then find a way to get away without them following. Instead he followed his gut. He glanced up at Bates and Franks who waited for an answer.

"It was Kerchief; he has Cayce with him," he stated.

Bates and Franks looked at one another. "Don't get any ideas about going after her alone Jonas," Bates commented. "It's too risky and more than likely a trap to capture you. We can figure out a way to get her back."

Jonas shook his head. "No. Trap or not, I'm going alone. It's me he wants, so I've offered myself in Cayce's place. I must go alone; if he spots anyone else, he will kill her. Get the remaining hostages back to Mahoney and let me go."

Bates glanced over to Franks. "I know I'm not the person you answer to," he stated to Jonas, "but I've got to insist we help you. My team and I can transport you to within ten miles and drop you off just outside of Al-Kasrah. With Jeff's help, we can go unnoticed while keeping in touch with you if things go wrong. Come on, man; think about it. I can't just let you go alone."

Jonas quietly stared out the roll-up door into the small town deep in thought. "I'll go along with it under one condition: you do not - I repeat do not - enter the compound unless Cayce's life is in danger. I don't care about mine, but if she is in danger, get her out!"

Bates nodded in agreement. "It's your call."

"Right now I have unfinished business to attend to, so excuse me," Jonas stated as he turned back to the enforcer. He had previously implanted a word that would cause the enforcer to see things as they really were, and he was about to speak that word.

He turned towards Bates, Franks, and the rest of the team. "I need everyone to stay clear and be ready for anything." Everyone glanced at each other, uncertain what Jonas meant. He turned back to the enforcer and simply stated the word: *"Coward!"*

As if waking from sleep, the enforcer stopped babbling and bowing, and he slowly raised his head. Fear filled his eyes as he realized that Jonas was not Allah.

He scanned the immediate area where he knelt and noticed his knife and sheath merely feet away from him. Jonas waited, wanting him to go for it. The enforcer's eyes shifted around the room, and in a flash he lunged towards the knife.

Everyone's weapons snapped towards the enforcer as he got to his feet, knife in hand. Jonas stood with his arms straight out to his sides.

"No, he's mine!" he stated, and the weapons reluctantly lowered. He dropped his .45 to the floor and reached down to pull out a ten-and-one-half-inch Bowie knife that was strapped to his right leg.

The enforcer's eyes dropped to the blade and shot back up to meet the glare on Jonas's face as they began to circle one another.

XII. Al-Kasrah

Mahoney could not stand it anymore; the silence on the radio was deafening. He had to know what was happening. It had been too long since the last contact.

He grabbed the mic and called out. "Team three, team one or two? Do you copy?" Silence responded. He was just about to call again when team one responded.

Mahoney drew a sigh of relief. "Team one, what is your status?" he asked as a bead of sweat rolled down his brow.

After a few seconds, the radio operator responded. "Hold on, sir. I will get you Captain Bates." A long stretch of silence followed as he waited.

Bates and Franks watched as the intensity increased between Jonas and the enforcer. They each took swipes at each other with their knives, trying to feel each other out.

The radio operator approached Bates and announced that Mahoney was on the horn requesting a status.

"Shit! I forgot to call him," Bates said to himself and nudged Franks to get his attention. "If he even looks like he's losing, waste that camel jockey. Got it?" Franks nodded his understanding as Bates and the radio operator headed outside the warehouse door.

Outside, Bates grabbed the mic and responded to Mahoney.

Almost at once Mahoney responded. "Captain Bates, you guys have got me climbing trees out here. What the hell is happening?"

Bates drew in a deep breath and collected his thoughts. "The compound is secure, as well as four of the hostages. Unfortunately, we found two DOA's when we arrived and one missing. We think the missing hostage was taken in a black SUV when it departed the compound. I'm sorry to say that the hostage was Miss Cayce, sir."

"Damn it to hell!" Mahoney blasted out in frustration. "We had them dead to rights. What tipped them?"

"Not sure sir, but they knew we were coming; that much was for certain," Bates responded. "I'll be sending one of our trucks back with four of the team along with the remaining hostages, and the bodies of the two. We - meaning what is left of the team and myself - will then go ahead with the other truck after Kerchief. Is there anything else that you need from me at this point sir?"

"No, you and the teams have done well. I need to get on the horn to my contact. Damn it! We need to track down that black SUV. I sure as hell hope he's not headed for Al-Kasrah. Our government has finally gotten off its ass and is sending in an air strike, it will be there in less than an hour. If he's taking Cayce there, I'll be in touch." Mahoney stated and cut the conversation.

Inside the warehouse, the battle had progressed. Jonas had managed to cut the enforcer's left forearm, while the enforcer had managed to cut Jonas on the upper leg. They were locked in battle, each trying to gain the advantage.

Suddenly in one swift move, the enforcer rolled backwards, pulling Jonas over top of him as he hit the floor. Using his knees, he pushed Jonas over his head and they lay flat on their backs, head to head.

By the time the enforcer got back to his feet, Jonas was on all fours and charging him. The impact knocked the enforcer backwards into the air and jarred the knife loose from his grip. He slammed his back on the floor hard, and before he could recuperate, Jonas was on top of him.

Jonas straddled the enforcer, and with both hands on the hilt of the knife, he pushed with all his might, aiming to stick the knife into his throat. Little by little, the enforcer began to weaken, and the blade moved closer to his throat.

The enforcer began to chant something in Arabic, continuing until the blade entered his throat. He choked on his own blood before his body went limp.

"This one is for Cayce," Jonas roared. *"And this one is for Crawford."* He made a quick jerk of the blade to the right, causing his partial decapitation.

Bates re-entered the warehouse, and was shocked by what he saw. "Well, I guess he didn't need help," he mumbled to himself and turned to Franks. "That man has got a lot of anger issues bottled up inside him. I would hate to be Kerchief when he catches up with him."

Within minutes, the truck with the hostages loaded and pulled out. Bates sent two of his own men to safeguard them back to Mahoney, along with Marcy and Aljeb. The rest of the team loaded into the second truck and headed in the direction the black SUV, skirting the edges of the town.

Bates knew from experience not to venture through the town. The terrorists fled there and into hiding when shit got deep; there was no need to risk it.

Jeff began to scan for possible contacts while Jonas and Bates discussed options.

"We are not going to have much in the way of options," Bates began. "Even moving at max speed, it will take us at least forty to forty-five minutes to reach Al-Kasrah, and that's taking you all the way there. It would only leave ten to fifteen minutes before the air strikes hit. Dropping you off ten miles out… you'll never make it in time."

Jonas contemplated what Bates stated. He had already surmised the same conclusion after finding out about the air strikes and had yet to come up with a plan that would work. If he let them take him all the way in, he would risk Cayce's life. Likewise, if he did not, he still risked her life.

After thinking on it, he finally responded to Bates. "What do you think the chances are that we could delay the air strikes? Not very long; just enough for me to get there and free Cayce. I don't care if I get out or not."

Bates glanced at Jonas. "This girl, she really means a lot to you?"

"She means everything," Jonas retorted.

Bates nodded. "Well, I guess the only way we're going to find out is to make a call to Mahoney, and see what he and his contact can do."

Mahoney had been on the horn with Davy and the current president, James R. Constance, for over fifteen minutes trying to get the air strikes delayed, but it seemed too late to make any changes to the plan.

The F-18's had left Ramstein Air Force Base and were nearly a third of the way to target. Calling them back would not only delay the mission, it would also in effect cancel it.

They discussed the idea of flying them around for an extra fifteen minutes to give the rescue team time, but it would still cancel the mission due to inadequate fuel capacity of the aircraft.

The argument now was to either cancel or go ahead with the mission. Each had a valid point, and each party was headstrong in their opinion, but time was running too short for debates, and Mahoney needed to act.

"Gentlemen, please can I have your attention," he broke into the conversation. The squabbling stopped. "I understand each of your points, but we don't have time for this. An agreement has to be reached. Time is short, and I'm afraid you have left me no other choice. I have made up my own mind and I'm sending my team in. If the mission continues, my team will be at risk, but my priority is to save the hostages."

President Constance became irate and began yelling into the phone. *"I order you to cease and desist in this operation Colonel Mahoney. How dare you give me, the President of the United States, such an ultimatum! I order you to call off your team."*

"I'm sorry sir," Mahoney responded in a calm, controlled tone, "but I am no longer in the employ of a sitting president, and if necessary I will resign my commission. I will do as I see fit for my team and the wellbeing of the hostages. If you chose to continue with the air strike and I lose my team and or the hostages, I assure you sir that I will make sure the world finds out about it."

"Mr. President," Davy cut in, "during my term, I had Crawford and the Stargate team under a presidential finding to help in the fight against terrorist efforts. During that time they continuously earned my respect and trust in these situations. This nation can never repay them for the acts of terrorism that they foiled during my time as president. I think this nation owes them. As a former president, I ask you to call back the air strike, and as a friend I ask because the hostage is my niece."

There was a moment of silence before President Constance replied. "I see why you're so involved in this John and you as well Colonel. I'll tell you what I'll do: I'll call them back to Ramstein, but it will only be to refuel and relaunch. This should give you, under my estimates, around two hours and fifteen minutes to get there and get out before they return and strike the compound. If by chance your team is not out, then I'm sorry. It's the best I can do."

Both Davy and Mahoney thanked the president, and before he hung up the phone, the president made one last statement. "By the way Colonel, I do not accept the resignation of your commission. I view you as too much of an asset to let off that easily."

"Thank you sir. Sorry about the threats, but I felt it necessary at the moment," Mahoney replied.

"No problem this time, but let's not make a habit of it... ok?" the president countered in a less than serious tone.

Jonas and Bates reached the decision to call Mahoney and plead their case. Jonas picked up the radio, ready to key the mic when Mahoney's voice rang out. "Team three, team one!"

Jonas glanced over at Bates bemused. "And he's not even psychic!"

Bates grinned. "You must be rubbing off on him!"

Jonas keyed the mic and responded, "Team one, copy."

"Team one, I have an update on the situation, and current status on the air strike." Mahoney began. "As of right now you have exactly two hours to get to Al-Kasrah, get Cayce out, and, if possible, take out Kerchief. Cayce is the primary objective; get her out no matter what. Then - and only then – can you go after Kerchief. Bear in mind, the air strike has not been abandoned, only postponed. Two hours tops and you need to be out. Do you understand?"

Jonas glanced at Bates, who nodded. "Team one copies. Thank you, sir."

"Don't thank me. It was a group effort. Good luck, and for God's sake be careful. Team three out." Mahoney replied and ended the transmission.

Kerchief was minutes outside of Al-Kasrah. Cayce, still in the fetal position, lay in the back of the SUV, numb to what was happening. She was so far back into her own mind that she doubted she could ever return to her old self.

Upon arrival at the training compound, Kerchief ordered the commander to recall all troops in the area and fortify the compound. They took Cayce into the building where she was bound in the large center room.

Unfortunately, Kerchief was not a strategical thinker and truly lacked training. Although, it seemed overkill to fortify the compound for one man, he was frightened of Jonas and his abilities.

Never in his life had he encountered a man with such talent, and it shook him to his core. He would not take any chances, nor leave himself vulnerable to his powers of suggestion. He summoned the lone enforcer to scan and make sure Jonas was not trying to impose his will on him.

The enforcer had psychic abilities, a fact Kerchief withheld from the others. This enforcer was his personal psychic shield and had proven to be much stronger in his abilities that all the others. That gave him a sense of security.

Closing in fast, Jonas, Bates, and the rest of the group were about to reach the drop-off point for Jonas. With an hour and twenty minutes left before the air strike, Jonas would need to run the remaining ten miles to save time.

He felt safe in assuming he could do it; he had found that running was a stress reliever for him, and he had continued running ten miles a day after leaving Stargate.

As they approach the drop-off, Franks leaned over to Jonas. "Be careful you don't step on any sand snakes or lizards. They're pretty abundant in this area."

Jonas glance back bemused by the statement. "Sand snakes? Lizards?"

Bates turned away to conceal a grin. "Oh yes, they can be pretty nasty if you're not careful. You see, the lizards hide just under the sand and if you step on them, they can bite right through a leather boot and take your toe right off just like that. But the sand snakes... they are the worst." Franks stated. "They also hide in the sand, and even though it's winter. If you're not careful where you sit, they can come right up under you, crawl up your ass, and cause heat stroke."

Jonas stared at Franks, uncertain whether or not to believe him. Bates could not hold it in any longer and burst out in laughter, Franks following suit. "You almost had me," Jonas replied as he joined them.

Jonas loaded himself with plenty of water and ammo for his .45 before leaving Bates and the group at the drop-off point. Will, Jeff, and Robert planned to stay in constant contact with Jonas as he proceeded, and if anything went awry, the group would move in without hesitation.

Bates worried that Jonas' mindset would cause him to become careless. It was his experience that when dealing with known terrorists there was always an ulterior motive behind their actions. He felt it was a trap, but Jonas was hell-bent on doing this, and doing it his way.

They would give Jonas a fifteen-minute head start before following him. The land in the area was flat, with very little to conceal himself. Most of the going would be on foot.

With then thirty minutes, Kerchief had the training compound secure and ready for Jonas, or anything else that might arise. His plan was to let Jonas enter the compound without any resistance. Everyone had been instructed to let him pass and direct him to the center building, at which point everyone was to close ranks and keep the building secure. One way in, and no way out.

Inside, Kerchief, the enforcer, and Cayce would be sitting in the center of the room, with eight of the top recruits. He wanted a heart-to-heart with this viewer man to make sure that he understood the conditions of his surrender and the swap, and if no agreement could be reached, they would both die. He had over two hundred men, women, and children armed and ready to do his bidding if it came to that.

"When this viewer comes, I trust you to keep me safe," Kerchief stated to the enforcer as they walked the boundary of the compound making sure things were ready.

The enforcer nodded. "It will be done. My life is yours my lord."

XIII. Aftermath

After hearing Jonas wanted to go after Kerchief alone and make a swap for Cayce, Mahoney popped a cork.

"What in the hell is he thinking? Yes, our goal is to get Cayce back, but not at the expense of losing him in the process. I'm glad you were at least able to talk him into letting you come with him," he said to Bates over the radio.

"Well, with him yes…but we dropped him off ten miles out and we need to maintain a safe distance so we are not seen. With that being said, yes, we are with him, but a long way off if anything goes wrong. I've got a very uneasy feeling about this sir," Bates retorted. "Very uneasy indeed."

"I see. Do your best and remember the deadline," Mahoney stated. "That air strike will not be recalled a second time. If he is not out with Cayce within a safe period to clear the compound, go in and get them. Do you understand? I don't care what Jonas wants at that point."

"Understood sir. We will be in touch. Team one out." Bates ended the transmission.

Jonas set himself at a steady pace and was making good time. Thoughts of Cayce flashed through his mind as he ran, continuously fighting back his emotions.

During the siege at the warehouse, he noticed how weak he felt after each trip he took, and he did not know why. He gave it very little thought, and shrugged it off exhaustion and hunger.

Unbeknownst to him, the white spots on his temples had more than doubled in size. His abilities - more so the endorphin overloads – began to have an effect on him, both physically and mentally.

Word came from the lookouts: a man on foot was approaching. He was still a ways out, but he was there. Kerchief finished giving final instructions to his men and went to the center building to wait.

Jonas had been running for six miles, and he was winded. Running in the sand was much harder than he anticipated it would be. He pushed onward; the compound became more pronounced as he got closer. He began to see people moving around inside the confines.

Fifty minutes later, he arrived at the compound gates. He was extremely winded and struggling to catch his breath, but he had made it. As he approached the gates, they swung open as he cautiously entered the compound. It was swarming with men, women, and children, each armed and staring at him with hatred in their eyes.

He had a very uneasy feeling about the place, and the feeling was multiplied by the reception. They directed him towards a building deep inside the compound where several guards were posted.

As he was about to enter, he noticed a young boy that could not have been much more than twelve or thirteen standing by the entrance. The boy glared back at Jonas with so much contempt, it sent a chill down his spine.

He wondered why someone would take such an innocent child and expose them to such horrors, stealing their childhood. It made him despise Kerchief even more, which he did not believe was possible.

Inside, he was taken to a large room in the center of the building. There sat Kerchief along with a taller man with a red beard and black turban. Just behind them, he saw Cayce, all balled up on the floor.

His heart dropped when he saw the condition she was in; so frail, dirty, and despondent. His eyes shot to Kerchief. If looks could kill, Kerchief would have dropped where he sat.

"So…Mr. Viewer man, I see you have made it, and just in time I might add," Kerchief boasted as their eyes connected. Jonas stood quietly showing no emotion as he continued. "I must admit, I wasn't sure you would make it on time, or come alone. It is a very foolish risk you take; this female must mean a lot to you."

Jonas listened as he scanned the room. Inside the room, there were eight men with weapons, along with Kerchief and the bearded man. He estimated a couple hundred within the compound.

He knew there would be no escape, and if Kerchief did not honor his word and let Cayce go, there would be no escape for either of them.

Bates and his team were able to move in about three to four miles out from the compound. They could see the compound was heavily fortified with troops and vehicles; they were definitely outnumbered and outgunned.

Mahoney was keeping them updated on the air strike and time remaining, but the deadline was closing in fast. In less than an hour's time, the strike would begin, and all anyone outside the compound could do was wait and hope Jonas was successful.

After moving within a mile, Bates split his men into two groups and covered the entire eastern side of the compound. With any luck, they would see Cayce coming out, and they would come out of hiding and retrieve her.

Jonas and Kerchief were still on the plate as far as Bates was concerned. If he could retrieve either one of them, it would be icing on the cake. He preferred Jonas; Kerchief would be a battle for another day.

Kerchief rambled on, blowing his own horn about the situation, and how smart he was to get Jonas to come alone. Jonas had just about heard enough.

"I didn't come here to hear you toot your own horn, and as far as that goes, you're not that smart. So how about shutting your mouth and let's get on with it!" Jonas bellowed.

Kerchief was bemused by the aggression Jonas showed. "As I see it, you are not the smart one. I was not the one who walked into an enemy camp alone hoping to retrieve and leave with a single insignificant hostage. I was not the one who put myself at risk; it was you."

Jonas fumed at the reference that Cayce was insignificant. Kerchief definitely hit a sore spot, but that was exactly what he wanted to do. If he could keep Jonas off his game, the odds were that his abilities would be less effective.

However, he had no idea that infuriating Jonas would stack those odds against him. He continued to egg on Jonas.

"You are in a bad situation my friend," he began. "You see, you have no way out of this compound alive, and neither does your female friend. By coming here you have in effect handed me what I wanted, and now the world will see how the Brotherhood deals with the United States and its agents."

That statement alone confirmed to Jonas that he did not intend to let Cayce free, and that he indeed was in a bad situation. He glared at Kerchief for a long second and shut his eyes. He pictured the eight men surrounding him as well as Kerchief and the enforcer.

He was about to try something he had never tried before, and he silently prayed to himself that it would work. He mustered up all his energy, all his pain, and all his hatred, and in one massive outburst sent it all out to the minds of everyone in the room except for Cayce.

Instantly, he felt an agonizing pain in his right shoulder as the eight men around him fell to the ground. The pain caused him to fall to his knees and grab at his shoulder. Shock struck him when he felt a large knife.

He opened his eyes to see Kerchief and the enforcer approaching him. He was in too much pain to concentrate on his abilities, and for a split second blacked out. However, almost instantly he regained consciousness as he was dragged across the room.

The enforcer grabbed the knife handle and yanked it out. Jonas let out an instinctive yelp of pain as the blade cleared his shoulder. He slumped over as he tried to regain control of his mind and the pain.

"Did you not think that I would be ready for your little tricks?" Kerchief questioned. "You gave too much of yourself away when you put your abilities on display. As you can see, impressive as they are, they can be countered."

He turned to the enforcer. "Take them and get ready. I will be there shortly. I want this finished; I have other places I need to be."

Jonas faded in and out of consciousness. For ten minutes or so, he fought to sustain a sense of where he was. The knife hit bone when it slammed into his shoulder, and came within an inch of hitting a major artery. He was losing a lot of blood.

Outside the compound, Bates worried that something had gone horribly wrong. The air strike was only twenty-five minutes out, and there was still no sign of Cayce or Jonas. He and his group slowly moved in closer as time slipped by, and they were with a half mile of the compound.

Bates and Franks decided it was time to make a move. Time was short, and per Mahoney, their orders were to get Cayce and, if possible Jonas, out.

Movement inside the compound lessened, and most seemed to congregate around the center building. They moved into position to gain the most from the weapons they had available, and prepared to move. Moments later, he made the call to attack; there was no more time to wait.

Jonas fought to clear his mind. He had to fight off the pain and save Cayce. Feigning unconsciousness, he let the enforcer drag him to another room, which appeared to be heavily fortified, and was forced to his knees. The enforcer said something in Arabic to someone else in the room and left.

He cracked his eyes open and saw two men gathering rope; they were apparently going to use it on him. He had no intention of letting that happen. As they turned towards him, his icy glare caught their attention.

They froze in their tracks as the pain thought hit them; they fell to the floor convulsing as Jonas got back to his feet. Ripping off part of his shirt, he wrapped his shoulder as well as he could, walked to the two men, and slit their throats.

He could hear commotion in the distance; gunfire and explosions erupted. Weary, he tried to make his way back to the center room, back to Cayce. He could hear Kerchief barking out orders. Following his voice, he eventually found the room.

Kerchief paced back and forth across the other side of the room. Neither he, nor anyone else, seemed to notice Jonas as he entered. It was not until he had made it halfway across the room that someone finally did.

Jonas was not sure what had happened when he sent out the pain thought earlier, but he was sure that it had to do with the enforcer, that he somehow was able to block it from himself and Kerchief, leaving them unaffected.

This time, before the enforcer realized it was happening, he hit him with as much pain as he could muster. As the alarm went out, alerting the others that Jonas was in the room, the pain struck the enforcer. His eyes flew wide open as he trembled. His eyes rolled into the back of his head and he dropped.

A panicked Kerchief pulled out a handgun and drew a bead on Jonas. Jonas was preoccupied with taking out the other men in the room; he did not become aware of it, until Kerchief pulled the trigger.

The bullet grazed the side of his head, and he fell to the floor. Kerchief turned and ran out the door before Jonas could regain his footing.

Outside, Bates and his team were making no headway and had suffered several casualties, including Jeff, who was seriously injured, and Walt, who had lost his life after taking several bullets to the chest while attempting to locate Cayce or Jonas inside the building.

The air strike was only minutes away. Bates knew it was a lost cause to try to get into the compound. Reluctantly, he gave the order to retreat. Shots continued to ring out as the sixty-caliber machineguns laid out cover fire.

Inside the compound, the people fell back to resume their positions, guarding the center building where Kerchief was holed up. Mahoney's voice broke across the radio. Both Bates and Franks stared at each other, and Bates answered the call.

"Team one, team three! Sorry sir, we couldn't get them out," Bates stated while Franks muttered, *"Damn it to hell,"* under his breath.

There was silence for several seconds before the reply came back. "Understood, you did your best. Mark the target and stay clear of the area." Mahoney's voice was thick with defeat as he spoke.

Franks pulled out the laser and lit up the center building with it.

Jonas did not know where Kerchief had gone, and he honestly did not care. He quickly finished off the other men in the room, turned to finish off the enforcer, and noticed he too had vanished. His attention shifted to Cayce who was still balled up on the floor.

He grabbed her by the back of her ragged shirt and dragged her as best as he could back to the fortified room. Still dazed from the bullet wound and unable to use his right arm, he was struggling.

The F-18's resounded in the distance as Bates, Franks, and the rest of the group awaited the outcome of the strike.

"It's in God's hands now," Bates stated as the first missile struck the building.

All hell broke loose as the building around Jonas and Cayce began to crumble. Explosion after explosion erupted; the ground shook violently as each missile hit its target.

Jonas moved Cayce into the furthest inner corner of the room, and used his own body to cover her as the chaos rained on top of them. Never in his life was he overcome with fear as he was in that moment.

He felt vulnerable and helpless, wishing it would stop, and in frustration, he yelled, *"Come on, you sons of bitches. I'm right here. Hit me, hit me!"*

It seemed like it went on forever, and he just wanted it to end. Suddenly, it stopped, and all was silent except for the burning debris around them. Jonas tried to move, but found that something had him pinned down across his back and legs. He struggled to shift his weight enough to get out from under it, but to no avail. He was stuck.

Bates and Franks watched as the F-18's laid waist the compound. Except for a few walls, the compound was flattened. Bodies lay everywhere, and fires were burning where buildings once stood.

After a few minutes, Mahoney called out over the radio to give the all clear. Bates and his team moved in to handle the cleanup and find Jonas and Cayce. They had little hope that anyone, including them, survived.

Bates and Franks took their teams and entered the compound, searching for survivors. Bates left his team and headed straight for the location of the center building - or what was left of it.

"Jonas! Cayce!" he called out, with no reply. He tried again, and thought he heard something. He repeatedly called out, trying to follow the sound.

He walked around in the rubble calling out, and then stopped. The muffled sound was close, but he could not see anyone, just piles of rubble and debris everywhere. He called out again, and to his surprise, just feet in front of him, he heard Jonas' voice.

"What the hell took you so long? Get us the fuck out of here!" Jonas yelled in frustration.

Bates glanced around and yelled to the surrounding men. "Over here, I found them!" He instantly began to remove huge beams of wood from on top of Jonas and Cayce. As the other men arrived, they began to remove debris until they finally got to them.

It took all five of them, including Bates, to lift the final beam off Jonas' back. They stood back in anticipation and waited while Jonas remained motionless. He had a large gash on his back and his right arm was covered in blood.

After a few seconds he began to move. Everyone rushed over to grab him and help. They laid him out face up on the ground. He immediately attempted to get up and started yelling, *"Cayce! Get Cayce out!"*

"Whoa there, cowboy." Franks attempted to get Jonas to lie back down flat. "We got her. She's being attended to right now, so stay put and let the medic take a look at you." Jonas laid back again, exhaustion taking over his body.

Jonas awoke an hour later to find that the medic stitched up and bandaged his back and right shoulder. He was bruised and sore all over, and had a hangover sort of headache to boot. Regardless, the first thing on his mind was Cayce.

He attempted to get up, but fell flat on his ass. The medic had given him morphine to deaden the pain while he stitched him up, and it was still lingering in his system. He swayed back and forth as his head swam. He tried once again to stand and failed. Giving in to the drugs, he sat long enough to clear his head, before crawling towards Cayce on all fours.

She was curled up staring into oblivion; her face was empty and void of all emotion. Jonas moved her hair from her face and fought the urge to weep. The lovely, sweet girl that he had met for the first time two years ago was no longer there, and it was killing him.

He took her into his arms, kissed her forehead. "Oh Baby! I'm so sorry, I'm so sorry…" he trailed off sobbing.

She was shaking from head to toe, flinching at every movement.

After several minutes, she slowly raised her head and gazed at Jonas. "J-Jo?" Her eyes widened, and as reality set in, she began grasping at him. Jonas felt his heart break and melt as his love for her overwhelmed him. He held her tightly and gently kissed her forehead.

"Yes, baby it's me. It's me, and you're safe now. I swear to you I will make them pay. I promise," he replied.

They sat on the floor in each other's arms and wept. Even though they tried to disgrace and humiliate her in every way possible, she was still his beauty, and always would be.

She had lost a lot of weight and was bruised from head to toe. Her face was almost unrecognizable. As Jonas looked her over, he took mental notes on her condition.

She was fading in and out of consciousness and needed medical help immediately. He raised his head and turned to Bates.

"Captain Bates?" Bates walked over to where he and Cayce were sitting. "Take her back to Mahoney and get her help. If I'm not back by the end of the day, go without me. Tell Mahoney I said so."

Bates stood in silence and began shaking his head. "Wait just a damn minute! You're not planning to go after that son of a bitch alone are you? I can't let you do that Jo. That's a suicide mission, a one-way ticket. I can't let you do it. I mean just look at the condition you're in. At the very least let me and a couple of my men go with you."

Jonas slowly stood with Cayce in his arms and shook his head. "No, I have a debt to settle with Kerchief, and it's been a long time coming. It's my fight this time. Just take Cayce and go. Give my message to Mahoney, and make sure she is safe and taken care of. Please."

Bates sighed and shrugged his shoulders. "Alright, it's your funeral, but Mahoney's not going to be happy. What are we to tell her if you don't return?

How is she going to feel about this? It's not all about you Jonas."

Jonas handed Cayce off to him. "Just do it, okay? If at all possible, I'll be there before it's time to head home. If not…just tell Mahoney not to wait."

Bates held Cayce in his massive arms as he sighed in defeat. "Fine. I guess all I can say at this point is good luck." He turned to his men and ordered the confiscation and loading of a few vehicles. "Let's get a move on before they gather enough courage to come back." Within minutes, they were loaded and gone.

Jonas walked outside to see what vehicles remained in the compound. To the left, he found an old beat-up BMW motorbike with a sidecar attached. He turned the key and kicked down on the starter. She fired right up, and he shot off, north towards the city of Al Bukamal in Syria.

Kerchief had at least an hour-and-fifteen head start on Jonas, but the enforcer driving was starting to have a hard time controlling the vehicle, which had apparently been damaged during their escape. The steering had become sloppy; the driver could barely maintain control.

Jonas on the other hand was gaining time fast, pushing the bike to its limits at full-throttle. The flat wasteland did not offer much in the way of cover. It was mostly a winding twisting dirt road used to connect the lower townships with the main paved highway.

There was at least a five- mile line of visibility in any direction; he was bound to be seen unless he stopped and hid behind a dune, which was not foolproof cover.

Kerchief knew he only had one chance: to make it to Al Bukamal before anyone caught up to him. He also knew that with his current vehicle, those chances were slim.

XIV. Payback

Mahoney, received word that the hostage was secure and motorized, and relayed the message to the former president.

"Is Cayce alright?" he asked, choking out the words.

"Yes sir," Mahoney replied. "She's a little beat up and traumatized, but she's alive. They should return here in about two to three hours. I'll inform you when we have them here sir."

Davy thanked Mahoney and the team for an outstanding job, and paused for a moment. "Did we lose anyone?"

Mahoney hesitated. "Yes sir. We lost one of our psychics and two from Captain Bates' crew. We also lost Jonas, our remote viewer. He's gone rogue after Kerchief. We can't wait for him to return, so he's on his own.

After a moment of silence, Davy added, "Please let me know when you're in the air."

"Yes sir, I will," Mahoney replied.

The rough dirt road caused the stitches in Jonas' shoulder to tear, and he was once again bleeding down his arm. The shot of morphine had also worn off, and the pain came rushing back full force.

He could not let the pain or blood stop him from catching Kerchief. If Kerchief was able to place the call to his sleepers in the United States before he stopped him, many people could lose their lives. He could not let that happen.

Kerchief and his driver were came to an old abandoned village about 25 km north of Jonas' location. The enforcer kept his foot on the gas as they entered the village, and mid-way through a stray dog streaked out in from of them.

The enforcer instinctively slammed on the brakes and swerved to miss the canine. Unfortunately, the stress of the sudden braking in combination with the turn caused the idle arm on the steering to fail. Both of the front wheels turned outward, and the SUV plowed to a stop.

"You fool! What have you done?" Kerchief blasted and quickly got out of the SUV to evaluate the damage. Seeing the condition of both tires, he took out his cell and started dialing numbers. One by one, he pushed end on his cell after getting no reply.

Finally, after the fifth try he got a response. "I am in a small abandoned village north of Al-Kasrah, about 40 kilometers or so. Hurry; I am in the open out here."

The enforcer attempted to come up with a solution to the steering problem so they could continue, but the vehicle was beyond repair. "Come!" Kerchief commanded. "We must prepare in the event someone has followed us."

They walked to the nearest shack and kicked open the door. The inside was empty, the roof had holes in it, and papers and trash littered the whole place. "We will wait here; someone will come soon." He just hoped it was not Jonas.

Jim Stafford and his team at the NSA placed an alert on the number that Kerchief used to send the text messages, and placed alerts on the numbers he had sent the messages to. It was doubtful Kerchief would reuse the same number to call again, but they would monitor it anyways to be safe.

All incoming calls to the United States from anywhere in the Middle East went through the NSA satellite system and fed into the computers for analysis. If anything even remotely identified as a possible coded message, it would be flagged and an alert issued.

Bill Winters and his FBI group, along with Homeland Security, the NSA, and local law enforcement across the nation, were able to track down several suspected members of the Brotherhood by tracing the cell numbers that had received the messages from the towers they last pinged.

It was not much to go on, but it netted a handful of suspects that otherwise would still be out there. They knew there were more, but they could only get what they had time and resources for.

Jim knew he had to ensure the country would be informed and ready. It would only be a matter of time before he needed to make the call to the president, updating him on their activity so far. He hoped before then, he would have good news for him.

An hour passed since Kerchief placed the call for help, and he was getting impatient. He knew that if someone was following, they would close in on him soon, which concerned him.

The enforcer stood in the doorway with his eyes closed, concentrating on any feeling or connection he could, but so far had not found anything.

Jonas had a gut feeling that Kerchief was ready and waiting for him. Hiding himself both physically and mentally, would give him much more of an advantage.

The pain in his shoulder was excruciating. In addition, his arm and right side were once again covered in blood, and he was beginning to feel the effects of losing too much.

He prepared for a mental battle; if it came to a physical battle, he was sure he would not win it in his condition. The element of surprise was what he needed, but he knew there were no guarantees.

The main disadvantage of a mental shield was his inability to use his abilities while hiding his thoughts. Unfortunately, that meant he could sense them than they could sense him. That left him just as blind as they were. He would have no idea where they were, or if he was walking into a trap.

He had no way of knowing they had broken down just seven miles ahead of him and were waiting, but an uneasy feeling came over him.

It was more of a feeling of danger than anything else. He was not sure why, but he knew better than to ignore such feelings. Something was not right, and he needed to be cautious.

He slowed when he lost visibility, only feeling safe to fun when he could see a long way off. Before long, he was within four miles of where Kerchief and his enforcer were holed-up, and red flags went up inside his head when he saw the run down village.

It was nearly dusk, and Jonas waited. He wanted that element of surprise, and the darkness of night would ensure him of that. He had no way of knowing if Kerchief was there, but felt confident he was, and planned appropriately.

As the darkness fell, he slowly worked his way closer to the village, crawling at times to ensure he was not seen. At the outskirts, he could see the black SUV in the middle of the village, and he knew he was right. He needed to know where they were and if he had been successful in hiding his thoughts. Only time would tell.

Inside the building, Kerchief paced, wondering where in the hell his ride was. He pulled out his cell for the third time and hit re-send. The phone rang on the other end, but there was no answer.

Infuriated, he stuffed the phone back into his pocket and began cussing and throwing a tantrum. "Why must I do everything myself? I have no one I can rely on to get things done," he bellowed in frustration as he began to pace.

The enforcer was distracted by this outburst, and he stopped scanning the area. He turned toward Kerchief and stated, "You will always be able to count on me, lord. I will never let you down; my life is yours."

Kerchief stopped and glanced at the enforcer, nodding. "I know my trusted friend; I'm just frustrated."

Outside, Jonas heard the commotion coming from the building on his left. "Bingo!" he said to himself as he moved to the side of the building and listened. He could hear the conversation, and it seemed Kerchief was upset over only having one on which to rely. He wondered what he meant, having only heard part of the conversation.

He moved closer to the door, staying close to the outside wall. The enforcer faced Kerchief, not paying attention to the outside of the building. Jonas felt this was his chance. He quickly moved into the doorway, and instantly shot a pain thought into the enforcer.

The enforcer, caught completely by surprise, began convulsing. Kerchief moved away from the doorway and into the far corner of the room.

Jonas felt the enforcer fighting the pain wave, and returning it to him. He pushed harder into the mind of the enforcer, and the pain returned. Suddenly, the pain hit Jonas full force, and he fell back against the wall, stunned.

The enforcer clumsily got to his feet and grabbed Jonas' wounded shoulder. He let out a wail as the enforcer pressed into the wound, and the pain intensified. He was too weak for a physical fight, and before he knew it, the enforcer was in his mind.

He could feel him searching his mind for information, his weaknesses, and his abilities, anything to which he could gain access. Jonas could not let this happen; he could not let this man have his secrets. Somewhere deep within himself, he pulled up enough strength to free his left hand, which he used to grab the man's gonads and squeeze as hard as he could.

The enforcer's concentration broke, and Jonas felt him leave his mind. He hit him once again with a pain thought while continuing to squeeze. The enforcer yelped in pain as the full effect hit him. After a few seconds, his body went limp and he fell to the floor.

Without giving it a second thought, Jonas pulled out his Bowie knife and slit his throat. Jonas stood with his hands on his knees, trying to catch his breath, when he remembered Kerchief who stood in the corner.

Kerchief turned pale, and fear covered his face as Jonas inched closer to him. "Do you know the saying, 'be careful what you ask for?'" Jonas asked him. Kerchief shook his head. "Well, it means the difference between what you ask for and what you get are two different things." He paused. "This, my friend, is one of those times."

Kerchief turned his head from one side to the other, searching for a way out, but Jonas gave him no openings. "You are now going to pay for what you have done," Jonas stated, and sent a thought into Kerchief's mind.

Thirty minutes later, a group of thirty or so Turkish mercenaries entered into the small abandoned village. They found Jonas passed out and bloody on the floor of the building. In the corner, they also found Kerchief.

He had been castrated, his throat cut, and his genitals stuffed into his mouth as well as his broken cell phone stuck in his ass. Jonas made a real mockery of him, but he surely made him pay.

The Turkish group accidentally intercepted the Brotherhood members sent to retrieve Kerchief, wiping them out some 40 kilometers north of this location.

When they pulled out the next morning, they took Jonas with them. He was still unconscious and very weak, but alive.

Mahoney waited two hours past Bates' return time in hopes that Jonas would show. However, after the two-hour mark came and went, he had no choice but to order the former Stargate members to load up and head back to Kuwait City.

Bates and his team of mercenaries planned to back to Al Kasrah to try to locate Jonas. Bates agreed to stay in touch with Mahoney with updates.

Once they reached Kuwait City, the hostages received medical care, and after being deemed safe for travel, they left Kuwait City and flew back to the UAE, where they boarded the Gulfstream and headed for Heathrow.

By the time they landed back in the United States, word circulated about the death of Kerchief. Bates and his crew were able to confirm the rumors when they reached the village, seeing Kerchief and the condition of his body first hand.

"Damn, I knew it wasn't going to be pretty when he caught up to him, but he really did a number on this guy," Bates stated over the phone as he reported to Mahoney.

Bates and his crew continued to search for Jonas for another three weeks before ending their search. They heard rumors of a Turkish mercenary group who found an American and took him to the city of Arar in Saudi Arabia for medical treatment.

Nevertheless, upon their arrival, they found he had already gone, and there were no further clues as to where he went.

XV. The Brotherhood's Fall

Months passed, and still no word about the whereabouts of Jonas. In the month following his disappearance, another leader of the Brotherhood was named. However, forty-seven days after he took command, he mysteriously died from self-inflicted wounds.

Another leader was named, and two months later, he also was found dead from self-inflicted wounds. Members of the Brotherhood began to fear that they were cursed, and that their calling was not the will of Allah. Despite the rumors, the upper leadership named a third leader, this time keeping him hidden and under tight security.

The attack on Al Bukamal was put on hold after the death of Kerchief. Leadership felt the need to revise the plan and reorganize the Brotherhood before moving forward with the attack. However, being unable to keep someone in the leader's position, the attack was questionable at best.

Their only hope was to keep the newly assigned leader hidden and safe, constantly moving him from place to place. The stringent security measures put in place were intended to give him time to reorganize the Brotherhood, and thus continue with the planned attack.

Five months passed, and the leader was still alive. In another three weeks, with the reorganization of the Brotherhood complete, the attack on the city of Al Bukamal would take place. Far too many members had fled in fear during the time it took to get a firm handle on things.

Rumors circulated through the ranks of the wishes of Allah and doubt in the leadership. Things were very shaky. The attack would hopefully reunify the Brotherhood into a solid force once again. It had to happen.

Back in the states, Cayce was physically healed, but the psychological aspect of her healing needed more time. Doc was also healing, and working part-time, doing research and running tests. Work seemed to be the best medicine for him.

The other members of the team had also healed, and the former hostages were currently in therapy.

Mahoney re-entered retirement and returned to his home off the shore of Lake Michigan. He heard about the deaths of the leaders of the Brotherhood and silently wondered if Jonas had any involvement in their suicides. Still, he never received any news about Jonas or his whereabouts, only rumors.

The other members who accompanied Mahoney and Jonas to attempt the rescue dissolved back into the general population. Jeff vowed never to return; he had had enough of the hardships that came with the job, and he was not sure he could mentally handle anymore.

The attack on Al Bukamal was scheduled to take place in a week. Final plans were made for securing the city once it had been taken. Morale was at an all-time high as the troops received word that the attack was taking place.

In a final meeting before departure, something astonishing happened. During his address to the top members, the new leader suddenly became soundless and motionless. After a few seconds, he picked up an AK47 sitting on the desk in front of him, and opened fire on his generals. Once he killed everyone in the room, he turned the weapon on himself.

Outside the encampment, a shadowy figure lay prone on a large sand dune. After several minutes, the figure stood and casually walked away.

Morale took a nosedive when the troops got word of what had taken place. The entire upper leadership was dead, and with no leadership, the troops scattered. They no longer believed that it was the wish of Allah to carry on with their cause. The Brotherhood was effectively disbanded.

Word reached the United States about the fall of the Brotherhood, and soon after, it reached Mahoney. Several uneventful days past, until late one evening, Mahoney stood in his home, staring out the sliding doors overlooking Lake Michigan. The reflection of the moon danced across the water in a spectacular glimmering show of light and water.

Not knowing what had happened to Jonas ate at him. He felt that if Jonas survived, he would have contacted someone in Stargate. He sipped his cognac and reflected on the past year's events. He wondered if there was anything he could have done differently.

As he turned to place his glass into the sink and go to bed, he received an overpowering urge to open the sliding doors and walk out on the deck. Not knowing why, he obliged.

"Hello Colonel," a solemn voice rang out in the darkness.

He felt his body stiffen up from the initial surprise. Realization suddenly set in; he knew that voice.

"Hello Jonas. It's good to hear your voice. How have you been?" he asked without turning to face him.

There was a short moment of silence. "I've been better. How is Cayce?"

Gazing out over the water, Mahoney stated, "She's better. Physically she's healed, but psychologically, she still has her moments. She constantly asks about you Jonas. She wants to know if we've heard from you or anything about you. She'll be ecstatic to hear you've returned."

"I don't want her to know," Jonas snapped.

Mahoney, confused, turned to face Jonas. Instantly he noticed he looked as though he had aged ten years; his hair was completely white on both sides.

"What happened to you Jonas?" asking before he realized he did.

Jonas looked out at the water and up at the sky, and began to answer. "After I left Al-Kasrah, I headed north towards Al Bukamal. I knew that's where Kerchief would be heading. I caught up to him and his enforcer somewhere in between in an abandoned village. I really thought I was going to die there that night, that enforcer had my number. It was the first time someone had ever been able to get into my mind and probe at will; I was helpless to stop him.

"Luckily, I was able to free my good hand, and - shall we say - put him into a bad position. After he went down, I slit his throat and watched him die. I had almost forgotten about Kerchief standing like a scared child over in the corner. I was weak, dizzy, and about to lose consciousness, but I made sure he got what was coming to him before I did."

Mahoney nodded his head, "Yes, I got a report from Bates shortly after you had left. He and his team went out to try to locate you and bring you back. They searched for almost a month before giving up. At any rate," he said, "you did do one hell of a number on Kerchief."

"He got what was coming. I wish I could have caused him more pain than what I did, but as I said, I was fighting to stay conscious. Anyways, I guess I finally did black out, and when I came to, I was being transported back to Saudi, where I got the medical attention I needed."

Jonas paused, deep in thought. "During the next few weeks as I healed, I put a lot of thought into what I should do next. I didn't feel that heading back the United States and leaving things unfinished was the answer. It needed to end; someone had to try to put an end to the madness.

"So I left and decided to do what I could to make that happen. I trusted no one, and at first, I traveled alone. I found myself foolishly wandering the desert, not knowing where to go. I needed help whether I wanted to accept it or not."

Mahoney cut in and asked, "What made you think you could do it alone?"

Jonas faced Mahoney. He appeared so tired and worn-out. "If it hadn't been for me, this whole thing never would have happened. The existence and use of my abilities put Cayce at risk, got Crawford killed, and hurt so many others. I had to make it right, I had to see it through and make sure it didn't happen again."

"Now hold on just a minute," Mahoney stated. "I don't know where you get off thinking this was entirely your fault. We acted as a team, and as a team we accepted responsibility. No one person is or ever will be held responsible for the actions that took place.

"As for this past year, Kerchief was responsible, he made the decision to do what he did, and -"

Jonas cut him off. "Yes! He did make that decision, but why? He wanted me and my abilities, that's why. If not for that, Crawford would still be alive. Don't you see it's because of me?"

Mahoney put his hand on Jonas' shoulder. "Jo, it's not your fault. No one in the group will ever say it was. As for Crawford, I happen to know that he thought of you as the son he never had. He was proud of you and your accomplishments, and he would have told you that you can't hold yourself responsible for the actions of others.

"Oman, Shofar, Kerchief, and the entirety of the Brotherhood brought this on themselves. If not for our team and their abilities, they would still be doing it, if not with us, with someone else."

Mahoney paused. "I know Cayce would want to see you, and it would crush her if you decided not to go to her. It's your call, but I can't promise you that I will keep the news of your return from her."

Jonas glanced at Mahoney. "Understood," he paused. "You know, the people I met over there surprised me. I had this ingrown notion that they were all like the Brotherhood, but I found that most of them were hardworking normal people just like most Americans.

"My deep rooted hatred of all Muslims was a result of the Brotherhood; it blinded me to the point that I viewed all of them as the enemy.

"I was so wrong. If not for the regular people over there, I would have been killed long before I got the chance to finish. I owe them a lot. They suffered more than anyone else at the hands of the Brotherhood."

He turned back to the water. "You asked me what made me think I could do it alone. Once during a meeting with the president that the president,

Crawford said, 'Cut off the head and the body will die,' and it made sense to me. That's what I decided to do. I continued to sever the head until the body finally died."

Mahoney smiled. "So…it was you. I had a feeling it was."

There was a moment of silence before Jonas spoke. "I can't involve Cayce anymore. I'm too much of a threat to her. There will always be someone out there that will want what I have, and I can't put her in that situation ever again. I just can't."

"I understand where you're coming from," Mahoney sympathized. "Still, you should let Cayce have a say in that decision. After all it involves both of you."

Jonas shook his head. "No, its best I just disappear again. I'm better off to everyone that way." He turned to Mahoney and reached out his hand. "Please see that this gets into the right hands. I had Kerchief remove it from his phone before I made him shove it up his ass."

"Ouch!" Mahoney grimaced. "That gives a whole new meaning to the term butt dialing." He laughed.

He held a SIM card from a cellphone, and looked back at Jonas. "I'll get it to the right people. Thank you, Jonas. The world owes you a great deal of gratitude for what you have done. It has been an honor to serve with you."

"It was my honor sir, but I'd rather the world, or anyone else for that matter, not know I had anything to do with it. I think it's best that way," Jonas stated.

Mahoney stared at Jonas, took his hand, and shook it. "Well, that's up to you. It's safe with me. Should you need anything, and I mean anything at all, please contact me. Take care of yourself. My door will always be open to you should you feel the need to come back."

Jonas nodded before he turned and jumped over the railing. Within seconds, he disappeared into the darkness.

XVI. Home Again

Over the next couple of days, Jonas spent time alone. He drove past his old apartment and wondered if Joni was still lived there.

He headed to the shipyards where he had spent a lot of time giving thought to joining Stargate. Standing at the floodwall, he gazed out over the water and wondered how different his life would have been if he had not joined.

A lot has happened over the past three years, he thought.

Heading out of town, he past the Shade Tree Restaurant where he met with Crawford and Mahoney. The feelings that swam around inside his head when he left that meeting had him realizing that there was more to what was happening in the world than what was happening around him. He left there completely confused as to what he should do.

A while later he passed the coffee shop where he and Cayce discussed the meeting with Crawford and Mahoney. Finally, before reaching the city limits, he came to the old office of Dr. Cayce Markham.

He pulled the jeep to the curb and looked at the front of the building. He remembered how he did not want to go and fought with his boss about it until he finally gave in.

He must have looked like a fool sitting in his jeep with an enormous smile on his face when he remembered the first time he saw Cayce. God she was a beauty; she literally took his breath way when he saw her.

After a few minutes of reminiscing, he put the jeep in first gear and drove north out of town. He would spend the following day driving before reaching his next destination.

A heavy fog settled into the cool Appalachian Mountains. It was late fall, and the air was brisk. He could smell wood burning from the nearby cabins as it carried down the hollows and valleys.

Jonas made the left turn onto the muddy dirt road towards his small cabin. He was glad to be home again. During the trip, his thoughts constantly drifted to Cayce. He wondered if he made the right decision, if he was being selfish not to include her in his decision.

He could not help but feel guilty for leaving without seeing her, but he also felt he had no choice. God, he missed her so much. His heart would never be the same; she had been and always would be his driving force.

It touched his heart when Mahoney told him what Crawford said about him. The fact that he thought of him as a son meant a lot, but it was sad that he could not tell him that he thought of him as a father. He learned so much from the man, and hoped what he had done was enough to show him how much he cared.

He believed somewhere up there, he was looking down and saying, "You go boy," smiling as he did so. A smile crossed Jonas' face as he recalled the time he and Cayce were called into his office.

"He sure had the goods on us," he said to himself as he reminisced.

As he reached the clearing to the cabin, an alarm went off inside his head. He stopped his jeep, got out, and quietly walked to the side of the cabin. He saw a figure sitting in one of the rocking chairs on the porch, rocking back and forth.

Slowly, he pulled his .45 out of the shoulder holster. Cautiously and quietly, he began to round the porch. The figure stopped rocking, stood up, and turned. Adrenaline instantly rushed through him; his reflexes were ready to act as he pointed his weapon.

Shock hit him like a jolt of electricity. He froze when he saw Cayce's face emerge from the shadows. Dropping his .45 where he stood, they rushed toward each other and met at the foot of the porch step. He took her into his arms and held her, kissing her sweet face.

Remaining in each other's arms for several minutes, they caressed each other. He kissed her face over and over again, and without warning, Cayce abruptly stepped back and slapped Jonas.

Taken by surprise, he stepped back as a slow smile began to cross his face. "I guess I deserved that."

"Yes, you did!" retorted Cayce. "What makes you think you can make decisions for both of us? You can be such an ass at times."

"Would you have recognized me any other way?" he sarcastically replied.

She smiled and fell back into his arms, squeezing him tight. After a moment, she looked into his eyes. "I like the new hairdo. Something new you're trying?"

Jonas grinned. "Unfortunately, no. It's a side effect from too many endorphins. I'm not sure if it will return to my natural color or not. We'll have to wait and see."

"It makes you look distinguished. I kinda like it," she stated, smiling. "I'm not going to ask you what happened or where you've been. I'm sure what you've done, you felt you had to do. I'm just glad you're back and in one piece. I don't ever plan to be far away from you ever again, so you better get used to me being here."

She paused for a second. "You were the only person I thought of when they held me captive. I cried thinking that I would never see you again, or tell you how much I loved you, or ever have the chance to do this." She softly kissed his lips. "I prayed for God to take me."

She paused again in thought. "I have not spoken to anyone about this since my return. They tried to get me to talk about it, but I just wasn't ready." She swallowed hard before continuing. "When they raped me, I - I just wanted to die. I felt so dirty and degraded, and I cursed God for letting it happen to me. *Why me? Why?*

"Still to this day I ask that question, but now that you've returned, I realize I know the answer. It made me realize how much you mean to me, how you've pampered me, how you go out of your way to make sure I'm happy and taken care of by giving me whatever I want. I love you so much more than I ever could have imagined loving someone."

He gazed into her eyes, and for several seconds was lost in them. His heart was pounding so loudly he could hear it in his head. Finally, for lack of the perfect words, he said, "I see your hair is coming back in very nicely. Do you think it will be very long come spring?"

She gazed up at him bemused. "I think it will be at least shoulder length. Why do you ask?"

Jonas smiled. "Well…if we're going to get married in the spring, I would like for everyone to be able to tell which one is the bride in case you don't wear a dress."

Cayce's eyes and mouth flew open wide, and with a great deal of excitement, began jumping up and down yelling, *"Yes, Yes, I will. Oh Jonas, Yes I will!"*

They held each other tight and cried in each other's arms. He looked down at her and stated, "I have loved you from day one, and will love you until the day I die. I'll be damned if I let anyone ever take you away from me again."

"I don't plan on letting anyone take me away," she replied, a naughty smile crossed her face. "By the way, remember when you tripped into me when I was undressing at Stargate?"

"How could I forget? You were pissed at me for weeks."

"Well…not really." Her smile widened. "Do you know how many times I waited and hoped you would to trip into me?"

Bemused, Jonas shook his head in a quick manner as if trying to clear it. "What? Wait a minute, you mean you wanted, and were waiting for me to trip into you?"

She started laughing and took off running; he was able to quickly catch her. "You had everyone there, including me, fooled, and I got my ass handed to me from Crawford."

She tried to pull away from him again. "Well, did you expect me to own up to the fact that I wanted you to do just what you did?" He pulled her back close to him, and picked her up into his arms. He started up the steps to the cabin door, as snowflakes from the winter's first snow of the season, began to fall.

Preface
Fragments of Dark Souls

When it comes to psychological sickness of the mind, the names of Bundy, Dahmer, Gacy, Homes, Ramirez and Ridgway are some of the names that come to mind. Each diagnosed with severe disorders, and all synonymous with the words Serial Killer.

One by one they each paid the ultimate price for their sins, and one by one their souls were released from their bodies. However, do we really know what really happened to their souls? Did they fall to the depths of hell, currently rotting, or are they in purgatory awaiting judgement?

Brad and Samantha Court are a world renowned brother and sister paranormal investigation team. Brad is a paranormal investigator, and Samantha is a psychic medium. They work together to solve hauntings and sometimes exorcise unwanted spirits from establishments and have been very successful at doing so for a number of years.

Having compiled a mountain of research over the years, they also authored several books on the paranormal, and traveled the globe giving seminars to would be investigators and enthusiast. However, by doing this it limited their time doing what they really loved, and that was investigating. In the beginning, they took on whatever jobs they could get in the paranormal field, solely because they loved the work, and doing the research. But eventually, it became too much to handle, and they found the need to narrow down their investigations to only the most active sites.

Currently, they are planning a trip to investigate a site that has been investigated in the past by many other paranormal teams. Nonetheless, each time a new team investigates; it always shows a new aspect and never fails to get the adrenalin going. Brad could hardly hold back his anticipation for the upcoming event.

The West Virginia State Penitentiary in Moundsville is a long time haunt for most of its past occupants. Over the years, there have been many documented cases of the paranormal in many of the cells as well as the room that once held "Old Sparky," the electric chair.

Although, it would be their second time investigating this prison, it would be the first time they would have access to the room in which the chair was kept. Consequently, this added to the excitement of a second investigation at this location.

The United States Post Office was created on July 26, 1775, by decree of the Second Continental Congress. Since that time its motto has been, "Neither snow nor rain nor heat nor gloom of night stays these couriers from the swift completion of their appointed rounds." And on this day, July 26, 2015, two hundred and forty years later, the postal service lived up to its motto and delivered a gold embossed envelope to the address of the BSPI (Brad & Sam Paranormal Investigations) team.

The envelope sat in the mailbox for two days until the team returned from the Moundsville Penitentiary investigation. Upon their return Sam walked out to retrieve the mail and noticed the embossed envelope with no return address. Curious, she opened it, and inside she found an invitation of sorts. It simply read, "Mr. and Ms. Court, you are invited to take on a paranormal challenge designed especially for you. If this peeks you're interest, please call the number below for more information."

Glancing down to the bottom of the invite, she noticed a number, 1-000-456-4422. "That's an odd prefix for a phone number," she thought to herself as she walked back into the office.

Inside, Brad was going through the missed messages on the answering machine, and writing down names and numbers of return calls they needed to make. Sam entered the office and approached Brad while at the same time reaching out to hand him the gold envelope. "What do you think about this?"

Brad read the invite and then scanned the envelope. "No return address and no name… Interesting, don't you think?"

"Interesting and odd," Sam retorted and continued, "You don't think this could be some crackpot trying to make a name for himself at our expense do you? I know that dealing with the unknown is what we do, but this is a little weird. What do you think we should do with it? Toss it?"

"Well…" said Brad, "As the saying goes, it's only unknown until someone investigates it. I guess it wouldn't hurt to make the call and see what it's all about. We can consider and base our decision after speaking to whoever this is." He then reached over and hit the speaker on the desk phone and began dialing the number.

A Note from the Author

The Remote Viewer and personalities are fictional in nature. However, the story is based on facts taken from research completed by top scholars and military personnel over the past century. Though, I did exaggerate the abilities to some degree, remote viewing is a real possibility.

During true remote viewing, the subject attempts to visualize a target, and although he may see items or objects during this session, it is usually only partial pictures or images.

It has then up to the individual, or someone working closely with that individual, to place this information into a final picture of what is being viewed.

I wanted Jonas Lux to come across as a normal guy, working a normal job with an exceptional gift, though raw and unrefined in the beginning.

During his progress and comradery with his newfound friends, I needed him to take on a different persona with an emphasis on his hatred for the Muslim faith. This of course, was a result of the actions of the Brotherhood.

However, during his quest for vengeance, he finds that it was not the Muslim faith, nor the majority of its followers, that caused events to unfold as they had. It was the radicalization of that faith by others seeking their own fame.

In the end, this realization gave him the strength and willpower to finish off the Brotherhood and what they stood for, however complex it was.

Many people read books and other literature, and each person could walk away with a different perception of the contents, even though they read the same context.

As a result, we as human beings are subject to our own manners of perception, and with it, the lack of true understanding as it may have been intended.

With that said, I hope you have enjoyed my book and have at least understood the story behind the words. If you have not read Book 1, please do so. It adds a lot of meaning to this book.

Good reading and God bless.

www.ingramcontent.com/pod-product-compliance
Lightning Source LLC
Chambersburg PA
CBHW022004170626
46808CB00001B/285